THE
MISSION

THE MISSION

A NOVEL ABOUT THE FLIGHT OF RUDOLF HESS

JEROME TUCCILLE and PHILIP SAYETTA JACOBS

DONALD I. FINE, INC.
New York

Library of Congress Cataloging-in-Publication Data

Tuccille, Jerome.
The mission : a novel about the flight of Rudolf Hess / Jerome
Tuccille and Philip Sayetta Jacobs.
p.   cm.
ISBN 1-55611-199-1
1. Hess, Rudolf, 1894–1987—Fiction.   2. World War, 1939–1945—
Fiction.   I. Jacobs, Philip Sayetta.   II. Title.
PS3570.U233M57   1991
813'.54—dc20   90-55337
                                                                       CIP

Manufactured in the United States of America

10 9 8 7 6 5 4 3 2 1

Designed by Irving Perkins Associates

For Marie and Lucille

PROLOGUE

Saturday, January 30, 1965

THE GREAT PROCESSION wound its way slowly through Tra-
falgar Square beneath a battleship-gray English sky. Queen
Elizabeth waited up ahead in St. Paul's Cathedral with other
members of the royal family, the first time in history that a
reigning British sovereign had ever attended the funeral of a
commoner. The queen, dressed in a black Persian lamb coat
with a matching black velvet hat, paid Sir Winston a special
tribute by arriving before the coffin was carried into the
church instead of afterward, according to custom.

Outside the cathedral, the muffled beat of drums and the
shuffle of soldiers in glittering red uniforms accompanied the
flag-draped coffin of Sir Winston Churchill through the streets
of London. Tens of thousands of men, women and children
lined the route along the Strand to observe the cortege, which
began at Westminster Hall, where the body had lain in state
since Wednesday, and ended at the top of Ludgate Hill for
the ceremony in the cathedral. Millions of others throughout
the world watched the spectacle on their television sets.

Perhaps the most commanding figure inside St. Paul's—certainly one of the tallest—was that of President Charles de Gaulle of France, wearing a plain khaki uniform that in no way diminished his stature. He was joined by representatives of 110 nations, including six sovereigns, five heads of state and sixteen prime ministers. Former U.S. President Dwight D. Eisenhower's glowing tribute to his World War II colleague was broadcast on television inside the cathedral.

The ceremony started promptly at 10:00 A.M. when Dr. Michael Ramsey, the archbishop of Canterbury, strode down a side aisle with his bushy white eyebrows set off nicely against his flowing black cope. Eight Grenadier Guards, resplendent in red silks, lifted the coffin from its carriage and marched it slowly down the center aisle toward the altar. Behind them came Lady Churchill, veiled in black, escorted by her son Randolph and other members of the family. Sir Winston had requested that "The Battle Hymn of the Republic" be sung at his funeral to acknowledge his American ties. The hymn served as an effective complement to the medieval-gowned trumpeter who played the plaintive notes of the "Last Post."

Following the service, the body of Sir Winston Churchill was borne down the hill on Cannon Street to the Tower of London for a final tribute, then placed aboard the launch *Havengore* and carried upriver beneath London Bridge all the way to Festival Hall Pier. From there the remains of England's wartime prime minister were taken by train to a small village churchyard at Bladon, not far from Blenheim Castle, his family's ancestral home.

Sir Winston Churchill, who had died of a stroke the previous Sunday, was finally laid to rest in the waning hours of a damp and gray Saturday afternoon. When visitors began to file through the churchyard in the evening, the first thing to catch their eyes was a wreath of red roses, tulips and carnations that had been placed at the head of the grave by his widow. The inscription on it read:

"To my darling Winston. Clemmie."

Thursday, March 17, 1988

The town of Wunsiedel, West Germany, lies in the heart of Bavaria, not too far from Munich, about seventy miles removed from the city of Nuremberg, where Rudolf Hess was sentenced to life in prison on October 1, 1946. In mid-March the ground was still covered with a layer of wet snow, and the air was particularly damp and cold in the hours just before dawn.

The band of mourners—Hess's son Wolf Ruediger, a few family members and close friends—followed the burial party through the mist toward the open grave. There was no music. As the coffin with the remains of the last surviving member of Hitler's inner circle was lowered into the gaping earth, the mourners filed past and paid their last respects. A few tossed flowers onto the coffin before the grave diggers shoveled the earth back into the hole.

The entire ceremony lasted perhaps half an hour. Secrecy and caution had been the watchword to the end. By the time Ruediger and the other mourners filed through the late winter snow away from Rudolf Hess's final resting place, the sun was barely inching up above the eastern horizon, a hazy red disk obscured by the morning mist.

SEVEN MONTHS EARLIER to the day, on the afternoon of August 17, 1987, Rudolf Hess had been found dead in his cottage on the grounds of Spandau Prison in West Berlin. The prison warden who discovered his body said there was an electrical cord around the neck. Hess was dead after a total of forty-six years in prison, apparently a suicide, successful on his fourth attempt at the age of ninety-three. The funeral, originally set for August 26, had been postponed when a large group of neo-Nazis had interrupted the cremation ceremony in Munich. The demonstration had begun with a candlelight vigil outside the prison walls on the night of the suicide and had grown in size and intensity throughout the rest of the week. The body of Rudolf Hess had been hidden in an undisclosed location until the quiet pre-dawn funeral on March 17, 1988.

In taking his own life, Hess joined the company of Hermann Göring, Heinrich Himmler, Joseph Goebbels and their Führer himself, all of whom had chosen to end their own lives rather than face the wrath of the civilized world.

The final chapter in the life of Rudolf Hess closed on a wet March morning in 1988. But the questions regarding his mission to Scotland in May 1941, when his plane crashed in flames and he parachuted to earth, have—until now— remained largely unanswered.

CHAPTER ONE

May 1941

Rudolf Hess's home in Isartel, on the outskirts of Munich, was not an elegant one. He had poorly developed taste in furnishings and art, and little interest in culture despite his literary pretensions. In this regard, he was unlike Göring and some of the other top aides of the Führer who outdid one another in their penchant for sensual satisfaction. Hess was the most ascetic of the lot, motivated almost exclusively by his abiding belief in Hitler and the Nazi cause.

Ilse Hess was tending the garden out front when her husband's limousine pulled into the driveway. Hess did not wait for his driver to come around and open the door. As soon as the maroon Mercedes came to a stop, he stepped out onto the path, his glittering black boots crunching the gravel.

Ilse observed her husband proudly. He looked every inch the Deputy Führer of the Third Reich in his pressed gray uniform. Six feet tall and handsome, his body trim and muscular, his dark, bushy eyebrows running like a hedgerow above his eyes, he was indeed an imposing figure. Ilse wiped

1

the dirt from her hands and stepped forward to greet him.

"I have news, Rudolf," she said.

"Yes?"

"Herr Hitler called here personally, not more than an hour ago."

She could see anxiety mixed with anticipation flash through his dark eyes.

"And so?" he said.

"He wants to see you tomorrow at Berchtesgaden."

"Did he say what it was about?"

"Only that it was urgent," she said, "and very important that no one knows of the meeting. Martin Bormann has arranged for a plane to take you there from Munich."

Rudolf Hess stared at his wife for a long moment and said nothing. He allowed something akin to a smile to flicker across his lips, then he strode past Ilse and entered the house. She followed him inside and sat down beside him on the living-room sofa. Hess's face was grim and expressionless and he appeared to be deep in thought. After a moment she said, "Can this be it then, Rudolf?"

He did not answer her immediately, but continued to stare at nothing in particular. Suddenly, he turned to Ilse.

"It must be," he said. "Finally. I can't think of any other reason."

Could it be? Was the Führer really going to take his advice at last? Just the night before, the Luftwaffe had lost thirty-three aircraft in a bombing raid on London. Thirty-three! The losses were mounting every day. How long could such an intolerable situation go on? Stalin had to be chuckling with glee at the idea of England and Germany bleeding each other to extinction.

"Do you really think—" began Ilse.

"Not a word," Hess said. "Not to anyone. If this is why

Herr Hitler wants to see me, we cannot discuss it with anyone."

Finally. At long last the Führer was going to take his advice and let him go on his mission to visit his friend in Scotland. And why not? He alone of all the Nazi High Command was qualified for the mission. He alone spoke flawless English, entirely without an accent. He alone was on friendly terms with members of the royal family who could get word directly to Churchill. He had experience as a pilot in the First World War and could fly his own plane. No one else had the dedication and qualifications to undertake such a critical mission. The fate of the Fatherland and the Third Reich was in his hands.

"You were always the one the Führer turned to in the old days," Ilse said. Hess turned his head toward her and stared. Such intense eyes beneath the heavy brows. His passion for the cause had not diminished in seventeen years, ever since she had known him.

"Yes, yes, that's true," Hess said.

Ilse thought back to the early days when she was a young, attractive blonde, a student at the university in Munich. She had joined the National Socialist Party almost at its inception, seduced by the fiery rhetoric of Adolf Hitler, who had a way of inflaming everyone he spoke to with his passion. She had known Hitler before she met Rudolf, and it was Adolf who encouraged her to take an interest in the young Hess and, finally, to marry him. Adolf, she remembered, had some concerns about Rudolf's apparent lack of interest in female companionship. He seemed almost too passionately devoted to Hitler and the Nazi cause.

"Do you remember," Ilse said, "when I went to Landsberg to pick up you and the Führer in that battered old car?"

"How could I forget?" Hess said. A hint of a smile crossed

his lips. He had been the one who was closest to Hitler then, one of the original founders of the party. Right from the beginning he had known that Adolf Hitler was chosen by destiny to lead Germany to glory. And his own destiny was to follow close behind him, to forsake everything else and help the Führer fulfill his divine mission. He had even gone to Landsberg Prison with Hitler and helped him write *Mein Kampf* while they were imprisoned there. How close they had been in those days.

"It's tragic," Ilse said, her voice trembling, "how those . . . those . . ."

"Opportunists," Hess said.

"Himmler, Goebbels, Göring, all of them, replaced you in the Führer's esteem."

"They're opportunists," Hess repeated. "They would have no compunctions about betraying the Führer or the Fatherland itself, if it would feather their own nests. They flatter him, they lie to him, they tell him what he wants to hear. They blind him with their empty words."

"But you're the one he still turns to for advice when his back is against the wall," Ilse said.

Hess patted his wife's knee, a rare gesture of affection. Abruptly, he stood up, all business once again.

"Tell Karl to come in," Hess said. "There's much to do before tomorrow."

Ilse went back outside to summon Karl Pintch into the house. He had been Hess's adjutant, his driver, his general amanuensis for nearly a decade now. A moment later he was standing at Hess's side.

"Prepare for a short trip," Hess said. "And not a word to anyone. We're leaving for Berchtesgaden in the morning."

*   *   *

THE BLACK MERCEDES limousine traveled up a mountain road, through a thick, lush forest until it reached a heavily manned security checkpoint. The guards recognized Rudolf Hess and his adjutant, saluted smartly and motioned for them to pass on by. Further down, the road began to narrow, and the limousine halted in front of another security post. Once again they were waved on past. Minutes later, the dark Mercedes climbed the long, winding hill that brought them directly in front of the Führer's retreat.

Hitler's Berghof sat high up in the mountains above Berchtesgaden, surrounded by a majestic sweep of towering pines and snow-capped peaks. It was a country house built in the upper Bavarian mountain style, with a wide wooden veranda facing down the valley. Heavy rocks, placed on the pitched roof by order of the Führer, kept the shingles from blowing off in a storm.

Several buildings were carefully camouflaged with bushes and trees to deceive enemy pilots. There were barracks to house the SS troops on the site, dormitories for officers and large garages for the fleet of Mercedes Benz limousines. Within view of Hitler's Berghof were three smaller homes that had been built for Göring, Goebbels and Bormann, who were available—at Hitler's insistence—twenty-four hours a day. A barbed-wire fence enclosed the entire compound, which was also cordoned off by a tight perimeter of specially trained Gestapo troops.

"The Führer is expecting you," the Gestapo officer said, admitting Hess and his adjutant into the Berghof. Pintch was directed to the SS dining hall, where a number of officers were having dinner, and Hess was ushered into the main dining room, where Hitler and his entourage were waiting for him.

The large, square-shaped room was resplendent with antique china and French and Dutch paintings arranged closely along the walls. Each wall had a recess harboring marble statues of ancient Greek rulers. Glass doors at the rear of the dining room opened out into the garden. A huge, rectangular dining-room table occupied the center of the room, and the table was surrounded by comfortable leather captain's chairs at which Hitler and his guests were seated.

Hess clicked his heels and nodded first to the Führer, who sat at the head of the table.

"Ilse sends her warmest greetings and good wishes," Hess said.

Hitler smiled and nodded. He stared at his Deputy Führer with those dark eyes that never seemed to blink, then gestured toward the vacant chair beside him.

"You had a pleasant journey, Rudolf?" Hitler said.

"Yes, fine, my Führer," Hess said. "Thank you."

Seated at Hitler's left was Unity Mitford, who was said to be one of Hitler's mistresses. She was trim and blonde, with fine white skin, the daughter of Lord and Lady Redesdale, who were sometimes referred to as "Great Britain's First Family of Fascism." Her sister Diana was married to Oswald Mosley, the leader of the British Fascist Party. The Redesdale home in England was the headquarters of the so-called Cliveden Sect, a pro-Hitler group of wealthy British aristocrats who numbered among their members such worthies as Lord Rothermere, owner of the London *Times*, Lord Lothian, ambassador to the United States, and Lady Astor. The Redesdales boasted of a blood relationship to Britain's prime minister, Winston Churchill.

Also present at the table were Heinrich Himmler, who stared at Hess through horn-rimmed glasses with his small expressionless eyes; Reich Marshal Göring, spectacular as usual in one of his dazzling white uniforms stretched across the width of his 220-pound body; and the crippled, diminutive Joseph Goebbels, at whose home Diana Mitford had married Oswald Mosley, with Adolf Hitler serving as best man.

"You know why I have summoned you here, Rudolf," Hitler said. It was both a statement and a question, a disconcerting style that the Führer had of addressing people. There seemed to be a suggestion of a playful smile beneath his chopped-off mustache, but with the Führer one could never be certain.

"I . . . I can only surmise," Hess said.

"And?"

"I assume it . . . it has to do with my proposed mission, Führer," Hess said.

Hitler smiled openly now, and looked to his left at Unity Mitford.

"I understand you speak English quite well," Mitford said, addressing Hess in her native tongue.

"I was born in Alexandria," Hess said in English. "I played regularly with children from the British community when I was young."

"Ah, you are not German then, you are Egyptian," Mitford teased him. Hess, never one to respond well to humor, blushed visibly.

"Show him the map!" Hitler said. "Miss Mitford is on good terms with the Duke of Hamilton, your friend. We have here a plan of his estate in Scotland that I want you to study carefully."

So it was true—the Führer had decided to put his plan to work after all. The Luftwaffe's failure—Göring's fault, ultimately, since he was responsible for Luftwaffe strategy—to penetrate the defense forces of the Royal Air Force had finally convinced Hitler that defeating Britain would not be as simple a matter as Reich Marshal Göring had predicted. It was apparent to everyone by now that neither Germany nor Great Britain could win this conflict easily; both sides were destined

to destroy themselves in a no-win war, while Russia stood on
the sidelines observing the countries bleeding each other
slowly to death.

Having conquered all of Europe, Germany's goal of total
domination of the continent was being thwarted by the tenac-
ity and fighting spirit of Winston Churchill, who had rallied
his nation around him.

The madness had to stop. England and Germany had one
enemy in common: Joseph Stalin. Great Britain had clearly
allied itself with the wrong country. Surely, Churchill's un-
holy relationship with Communist Russia was one of
convenience—and seriously misguided at that. Hess's plan,
the one he had presented to Hitler months before—to fly
directly to Scotland and make contact with influential and
sympathetic British leaders—was Germany's only hope.
Churchill had to be convinced that England's own best interests rested with the annihilation of Soviet Russia. If Churchill
would agree not to launch an attack on Germany's western
flank while the Fatherland turned eastward and wiped out
their common enemy, then England and Germany could live
together in peace afterward. That was the only solution, the
only hope for the survival and future prosperity of both nations.

"The mission can succeed," Hitler said to Mitford in his
disconcerting manner.

"Hamilton will do his part," she said. "The rest depends on
Herr Hess and his navigating skills. Flying into Scotland at
night, penetrating air defenses, landing safely on the duke's
estate, all requires a certain—ingenuity, shall we say."

"Rudolf?" Hitler said.

"It can be done," Hess said. "As long as I am properly
equipped, my mission will succeed."

"Hermann will see to that," Hitler said.

"He will not have any problems," Göring said. "I can arrange to add extra fuel tanks to one of our standard Messer-schmitts. Also, special radiogram receptors to receive our signals. This can be done in two days, three days at most."

Hitler looked at Hess. There was no smile on his face and his eyes did not blink.

"You will compose a letter to me," Hitler said, "in which you will inform me of your lone decision to undertake this mission. The contents should bear evidence that no one knew of this plan but you. It was your decision and yours alone. If you fail, Rudolf"—Hitler paused for emphasis—"I will dis-avow any knowledge of it. Present this letter to your adjutant the day you leave, and instruct him to deliver it personally to me here. Understood?"

"I understand, my Führer."

"If you succeed in getting through," Hitler said, "contact us through our agents in Portugal. Under no circumstances should you try to reach us directly."

"Yes, my Führer."

"If you accomplish your goals," Hitler said, "the entire Fatherland will owe you an incalculable debt of gratitude."

"Thank you, Führer."

"And if you fail," Hitler said, "your mission will go down in history as the journey of a madman."

And if, my Führer, this project ends in failure, and the fates decide against me, it will always be possible to deny all re-sponsibility. Simply say I was crazy.

Rudolf Hess entered this brief passage in his journal as his driver pulled into the driveway. Ilse was tending the garden in front of the house. He could see her wipe her hands free of moist soil on the sides of her slacks, her eyes large with ex-pectation as he stepped from the car.

"So?" she said. "Your meeting went well?"

"It is done, Ilse. I am leaving immediately."

"Willy called," Ilse said, referring to Willy Messerschmitt. "He is very anxious to speak with you."

"Call him back," Hess said. "Tell him only that I will see him at his factory tomorrow morning. He'll know what it's about."

"Also, Herr Haushofer called," Ilse said. "He said it was urgent."

"Ah yes. Him I will call myself."

Hess stepped into the house and dialed Haushofer's number. The professor answered the phone himself on the third ring.

"I have good news, Rudolf," Haushofer said.

"Yes?"

"I've heard from Hamilton," Haushofer said. "A note in his own handwriting. He is anxious to meet with you and discuss your plans. Just tell him when."

"Reply to him immediately, Karl," Hess said. "Tell him I will be arriving at Dungavel Castle in a few days. He should be expecting me any time."

"As you wish, Herr Hess. May the gods be with you."

After speaking to Haushofer, Hess called in his secretary and dictated a letter to the Führer along the lines they had discussed at Berchtesgaden. The letter was dated May 8, 1941.

"Send the original and keep only one copy for my files," Hess said.

The following morning, a brilliant sunny day with a cloudless canopy of blue sky, Rudolf Hess was driven out to Augsburg to meet with Willy Messerschmitt. Messerschmitt, a tall, regal man with a forbidding presence, greeted his guest with all the warmth he could muster, and took him at once to see the specially built aircraft he would be flying.

"It is designed precisely according to Göring's specifications," Messerschmitt said.

"Oh?"

"It is stripped bare, designed to outmaneuver the British Spitfires, which have a reputation for somewhat greater speed—undeservedly, I might add. Of course we had to make some modifications."

"What sort of modifications?" Hess asked.

"It is lighter than usual, and the cockpit is a bit more compact." Messerschmitt attempted a smile as he studied Hess with amused curiosity. "That should pose no problem for a man of your athletic fitness, but I suspect a man of Göring's, uh, stature would find it a tight squeeze. In any event, you will have enough fuel to get you to your destination, and the radiogram receptor will keep you on course when you need to orient yourself. This is quite a remarkable achievement on such short notice."

Hess studied the aircraft fondly, admiring the sleek lines and finely honed efficiency.

"When will the final touches be ready?" he asked.

"This evening perhaps, tomorrow morning at the latest." Messerschmitt lifted both arms in the air as if to say, the rest is the hands of the gods—and the skilled hands of the pilot.

HESS SPENT THE evening memorizing his maps and preparing himself psychologically for his mission. He retired early and slept well, as he had disciplined himself to do over the years, no matter what adventure awaited him in the morning.

He awoke at dawn, dressed quickly and ate a light breakfast of biscuits, jam and strong Italian coffee. He was as ready now as he'd ever be, ready to accomplish his mission for the Führer, for the Reich, for the glory of the Fatherland.

His aircraft responded instantly to his touch, a feather-weight version of anything he had flown before. He was up and off, away beneath the sprawling German sky. His escort, two ME-109s, followed him part of the way, more to wish him well on his curious winged adventure than to protect him from anything that could do him harm. They dipped their wings in respect, then peeled away to the right and to the left.

And then he was alone, a solitary pilot headed westward toward the sea on a mission that would change the direction of the war, that would alter the very course of human history.

CHAPTER TWO

THE WEATHER REPORT for Scotland on May 10, 1941, called for light rain and fog over the Scottish lowlands. By nine o'clock in the evening, the sun had recently set and the pilot increased his altitude and speed as he approached the coast to avoid becoming an easy target for British Spitfires that would most likely be patrolling the area. He thought the incipient darkness and low visibility would provide him with the cover he needed.

No such luck. He heard the droning through the mist before he actually saw them. Spitfires at three o'clock, directly to his right. He climbed higher, veered left, tracing bullets from the British fighters lighting up the mist. He continued to climb, but the weight of the extra fuel tanks slowed his normal rate of speed and he could hear the Spitfires gaining as they closed from beneath him. Suddenly, it occurred to him: The extra weight was a liability as he ascended, so why not use it to his advantage?

Hess pushed forward on the controls, leaning hard with all

his weight. He pulled back on the throttle, cutting his speed drastically as the Messerschmitt dove nose first toward the earth. His aircraft shuddered, then nearly blew apart as a shell from one of the Spitfires caught him in the tail. He plummeted toward the ground, his plane little more than a projectile out of control as it fell at blinding speed in a downward spiral.

Then he was below the fog, and he could see the dark gray contours of earth rushing toward him in a terrifying blur. He pulled back on his controls and pushed the throttle forward to gain more speed. Would the Messerschmitt respond? How much damage had the Spitfire inflicted on his aircraft? How much time was left before he smashed into the rocky Scottish lowlands?

Miraculously, the Messerschmitt responded to his command. The airplane leveled out, the shuddering decreased, and he was once again flying in control, though a bit too close for comfort above the treetops. Was he out of danger now? The droning of the Spitfires was no longer audible. They were nowhere in sight. Just where was he anyway? Safely inland, away from the heavily patrolled coastline? Or still in mortal danger of being gunned down by enemy fighters?

Hess had committed to memory the topography of the land from the maps the Führer had shown him, as well as the landmarks he should look for as he got closer to Dungavel Castle, the Duke of Hamilton's estate. The weather had improved as he moved westward away from the coast, but darkness had fallen and enveloped the land below. To his advantage, he was able to pick up once more the radio signals beamed from Augsburg to a point in Glasgow, which told him he had somehow remained on course despite his confrontation with the Spitfires. His fuel supply, thanks to the extra tanks that had been attached to his aircraft, was sufficient for him to complete the journey.

From his charts, he estimated that he was somewhere in the vicinity of Hamilton, just east of Glasgow. He descended once again, and tried to pick out the hedgerows that undulated around the estate, but the earth was totally cloaked in darkness. German intelligence, with the help of Mitford and the Cliveden group, had informed the duke of his mission. The pilot had been assured that he would have no trouble landing his aircraft. The duke had built a private landing strip on his land, and presumably would have it lighted up at this hour in anticipation of his arrival. But where was the landing strip? Where were the torches along the runway? Where were the lights from the duke's house that should have been glowing in the darkness?

Hess descended further, and circled over the area in search of something recognizable. The drone of his Messerschmitt should have alerted the duke by now that he was directly overhead. Surely, he should have heard it and turned on the lights so his guest could land safely. Then he saw them, lights from a house in the distance—the Duke of Hamilton's mansion, no doubt. Hess flew toward them, over a rooftop, and then he could see the markings of two Royal Air Force vehicles in the driveway. He had to find an open level field as soon as possible. Where was the landing strip? He reduced his speed and started to descend lower when . . .

He realized too late that he had reduced speed too much. Hadn't he been warned by Göring—that buffoon, he should have paid more attention to him—that he needed to compensate for the weight of the extra fuel tanks? At forty-seven years of age, Hess had never jumped out of a plane before, but he knew that he had no other option. He was barely 400 feet above the ground, too close to parachute safely. Not to jump meant going down with the plane to a certain death.

He heard the crash and saw the blinding volcano of flame before he hit the ground himself. The entire countryside seemed engulfed by fire. He didn't know it yet but—ironically, considering who he was and where he had come from—his Messerschmitt had crash-landed on the grounds of Eaglesham Country Club, the only Jewish golf course in all of Scotland.

Hess slammed hard against the earth of a nearby farm, and rolled over onto his side. A jolt of excruciating pain ran from his ankle into his leg, but he was still alive. At least he thought he was; if he could feel pain, he could not be dead. When he looked up he saw a solitary figure walking toward him across a meadow. Behind the figure, whom he quickly identified as a man carrying a torch in one hand and a pitchfork in the other, was a small, whitewashed farmhouse with a thatched roof. These were his first two impressions in the alien Scottish countryside: an ankle screaming with pain, and a man with a pitchfork looming over him as he lay helpless on the turf.

Resistance was clearly hopeless. Hess raised his hands over his head, and spoke in his best, accent-free English.

"Please don't hurt me! I am unarmed!"

He had reason to panic. According to the rules of war in his homeland—rules he had himself initiated—paratroopers were to be shot in the air before they touched German soil, even if they raised their arms in surrender. Many of them were armed with grenades that they threw at anyone who threatened their landing, and he had seen no reason to needlessly risk spilling the blood of young German soldiers. He did not know what rules of engagement governed the Scottish citizenry, but he anticipated the worst.

"I'm David McLean," the man said. "This is my farmland y've set down on."

Reasoning that he must get the upper hand right away, Hess said, "Take me to someone in authority at once! I must speak to whoever's in charge."

David McLean remained a few feet away—far enough to

thrust with his pitchfork if he had to—while Hess unbuckled his parachute. Then the farmer gestured for him to follow along toward the farmhouse.

The walk seemed interminable. Hess hopped most of the way on one foot, not daring to put much weight on the injured ankle. When he finally reached the front door, a woman who looked as if she were in her late sixties held it ajar and helped him into the house. There were coals burning in the fireplace despite the season, and she motioned toward a rocking chair in front of it.

"Some tea, perhaps," she said. She reached for the kettle on the stove, poured out a cup for him and placed it on the table beside his chair with a platter of scones.

The man—her son, Hess guessed—went to the phone on the far side of the room and spoke for several minutes into the receiver. Not once did he let go of the pitchfork in his right hand. Hess tried to listen while he drank his tea and ate one of the scones, but the farmer kept his voice low and his Scottish burr was impossible to follow from this distance. What strange people they were. They knew he was a German, a member of the Luftwaffe that had leveled Glasgow with bombs and killed thousands of its people, yet here they were feeding him tea and cakes while he warmed himself by the fire. Would he ever understand the workings of the foreign mind? Still, these were Scotsmen, not Englishmen in the strict sense of the word. Dominated by the English for centuries, they were not quite of the same race. With the English he could reason. With the English he could talk some sense.

The front door opened and two short, stocky men entered the cottage. They were both dressed in civilian clothes, but they wore white bands around their arms and white helmets with the word POLICE printed on them. He had been told to watch out for the Scottish Home Guards, a voluntary citizens' group that had been formed to assist the military.

"Aye, that must be him," one of them said. "It just came over the wireless, a single enemy plane crashed in flames. Are you the bloke then? Do y' speak English?"

"I do, yes," Hess said. Better than some of you, he thought. The men reeked of the countryside, hay, manure. . . .

"Tell us who you are then, if y' please."

"My name is Captain Alfred Horn. I have flown here on a secret mission and it is urgent that I speak to the Duke of Hamilton at once."

CHAPTER THREE

DESPITE THE IMMENSITY of Hitler's Berghof in Berchtesgaden, the Führer preferred to entertain visitors in his small, bleak first-floor study. He stood in front of his tiny desk, glaring at Göring and Goebbels under a single photograph of himself addressing a political rally that hung on the wall behind him. Rain drumming on the roof provided the only sound.

"You have the news," Hitler said.

"Not good, my Führer," Joseph Goebbels said.

"Is he alive?"

"Very much so. We don't know his exact whereabouts. He arrived at his destination, although not exactly in the prescribed manner. For some reason his plane crashed not far from Hamilton's estate. He parachuted safely and suffered only a slight leg injury."

"Where did you get this information?" The Führer downed his diluted wine and a cream cake in two gulps. Wine always soured his disposition. Goebbels sighed. Why was it always

19

he who had to deliver the bad news? Why did Hess have to crash? And if he had to crash, why not into the North Sea instead of Scotland, where the nosy English press were free to pry and ask questions?

"All the information comes from our embassy in Ireland," Goebbels said. While officially neutral, Ireland had been openly pro-German throughout the war. "The Duke of Hamilton contacted them with the news as soon as he heard. Churchill's foreign secretary, Lord Halifax, is in Dublin now, waiting to hear from us."

"And what are we to tell him? You have suggestions, please!"

Goebbels squirmed. Both he and Reich Marshal Hermann Göring had been summoned abruptly to Hitler's retreat as soon as the radio fix on Hess's plane was lost, and news of his spectacular landing started to trickle in. At five feet tall and 120 pounds, Goebbels felt dwarfed by the massive Göring, the current favorite of the Führer. He feared Göring almost as much as Hitler. The man was brutal and treacherous, his unpredictable moods aggravated by his growing addiction to various narcotics. As propaganda minister, Goebbels knew he was the likely scapegoat, the one expected to get the British to accept the cover story that Hess's flight to Scotland was the act of a lunatic operating strictly on his own.

As though reading his thoughts, Göring turned to Goebbels and said, "Has there been anything at all in the British press?"

"Nothing. We're monitoring their newspapers and radio broadcasts, and there's been no mention as yet."

"For how long?" Göring asked. He looked at Hitler.

The Führer sat down in the chair in front of his desk, then crossed and recrossed his legs in that curious female way he had—thigh over thigh instead of ankle on thigh like most men did it. He reached for his glass and tipped it onto the floor, spilling the contents. He stared at Goebbels without blinking.

"How am I supposed to present our story about Rudolf's mental instability to the English?" he said.

"So far his identity has not been disclosed," Goebbels said. "If Churchill is at all receptive to Operation Barbarossa, he will not be in a hurry to let the world know who Alfred Horn is."

Barbarossa was the name given to Hess's plan to have the British leave Germany's western flank alone while Germany invaded the Soviet Union.

"Yes! Go on!" Hitler stood up, ignoring the fallen glass. That narrow hacked-off mustache that he affected, his own interpretation of the gentleman English officer's, seemed to fill Goebbels's field of vision.

"Isn't that a trifle naive, Joseph?" Göring said. "How long can we reasonably expect Churchill to keep this secret from the British newspapers?"

"Hermann's right," said Hitler. "He must agree to our plan without appearing to be hiding something."

"Of course, of course, my Führer. I'm sure Churchill will make an announcement soon, before the newspapers beat him to it. Perhaps he will welcome an explanation from us about Hess's instability. It was a stroke of genius, my Führer, sending Hess himself on the mission instead of a messenger, as Hermann had suggested."

Goebbels looked sideways at Göring, who glared back at him without responding.

"As you agreed yourself, Führer," Goebbels, sensing a momentary advantage, continued, "a messenger would have been too risky. But Hess himself undertaking such a mission? Who would not believe he is mad? It is best he carried out his own plan. Now he is isolated. It is easy to distance ourselves from him. The story is entirely credible, and Churchill can accept it without compromising himself."

"I must know immediately which way Churchill is leaning!"

said Hitler. "Do we have any additional information from our intelligence sources?"

"Not as yet. Right now the British government's biggest problem is keeping Hess's identity secret—and explaining his presence there if the press discovers who he is."

"You're assuming that Churchill is interested in our proposal," Göring said. Goebbels glowered at him. The man had yet to offer a constructive solution to any problem. Why did Hitler tolerate such a boor?

"What do you suggest, Hermann?" asked Goebbels.

"Propaganda is your department, not mine," Göring said.

"All right!" Hitler said. "Release your story, Joseph. It's better that it comes from us first to avoid the appearance of a cover-up. Start preparing statements for the press at once. That's sufficient for now. We'll wait a day or two for Churchill to respond. Include in your statement that Hess has, of course, been relieved of his duties as Deputy Führer."

"Excellent, Führer," Göring said.

"As soon as Joseph releases his statement, Hermann, you will order the arrest and solitary confinement of Hess's adjutant, Karl Pintch. No one is to be allowed to speak to him."

"Wouldn't it be simpler to have him shot?"

"Not immediately. That would alarm the others who knew of Rudolph's mission. Pintch will be charged with failure to report Hess's mental condition and complicity in his flight. Meanwhile inform Ilse Hess and Willy Messerschmitt—at once—and warn them that their lives depend on their absolute silence."

"Shall I put them under house arrest?"

Hitler hesitated only a moment. "Of course," he said. "They are to be kept under constant surveillance, as is everyone else who knows of Hess's mission. I leave the details to you."

"Mussolini will want to know why he was not informed

eforehand," Goebbels said. "Perhaps Ribbentrop should be sent to Rome in person to massage the rooster's ego. We don't need another complaint about our doing things behind his back."

"He's more trouble than he's worth," Hitler said. "I'm tired of rescuing that fool from his own follies. I should have set Italy up as a friendly neutral like Spain."

"Unfortunately," Goebbels said, "the chances for the success of Operation Barbarossa are diminished because of Hess's accident."

"Perhaps not," said Hitler, giving his visitors a rare smile. "It could work in our favor after all. It *will* work. Churchill must act at once now, before the press demand for information gets too intense. Everyone will be demanding answers."

Goebbels waited for Göring, the perfect toady, to agree. He was not disappointed.

"This could be a gift from the gods," Göring said. "Hess's mission has been accomplished. He arrived at his destination and delivered his message, which was the purpose of his flight. The fact that it was not done in secrecy, and his identity is made public, is not necessarily an insurmountable problem. Our story is credible. The rest is up to the British now."

Hitler's smile, reflected in the reliable mirror of Göring's enthusiasm, was positively radiant. The two men seemed to share some kind of psychic connection that was nothing less than alarming to Goebbels, who still had high hopes of getting out of the Berghof with his neck intact.

"Do you think there's a silver lining in this affair after all?" he asked. "Can it really work in our favor?"

Hitler looked at him for a long moment. Goebbels looked away.

"Tell Heydrich to do the same thing he did in Czechoslovakia. Execute a hundred Poles, then dress them in German uniforms and use them as evidence of Russian atrocities."

With this reference to Reinhard Heydrich, deputy ̀
Gestapo, the Führer was almost bouncing in his ch

"At once," said Göring.

"We should begin now to shift air power to the Ru
front," Hitler said. He stood up and motioned for his ̀
deputies to follow him out of the room and across the hall ̀
his map room. Goebbels followed the others, as was his habit.
He didn't like Hitler to see him limping on his clubfoot.

A four-foot-long map of Europe hung on the wall. Hitler
picked up three pins with swastika-shaped heads from the
nearby table and stuck them into three Russian cities: Moscow, Leningrad and Stalingrad.

He was thinking of naming Leningrad after himself. After
all, he reasoned, it *was* built by German architects.

CHAPTER FOUR

Eaglesham Road was virtually deserted. The man who called himself Captain Alfred Horn rode in silence in the front seat of a Land Rover. As his driver approached the outskirts of Glasgow, he stared out the window at the small cottages with thatched roofs that dotted the rolling landscape every few hundred yards. He smelled the cool, damp air that carried the perfume of new-cut grass. Although it was close to midnight, the sky was still fairly light this time of year.

Hess felt his stomach heave as they approached Queens Park. His eyes shifted uneasily beneath his heavy brow. When the Land Rover stopped in front of the Victory Infirmary, a British soldier opened the door on the passenger side and motioned for him to get out. Once again he sniffed the air, turned and allowed himself to be led inside.

The room on the top floor of the infirmary was spare and clean. Hess studied the bald head of the rotund doctor who administered to his injured leg and wrapped it tightly with a bandage. Outside, the night was finally darkening a bit, but through the window across the room he could still make out the high hills and narrow streets of Glasgow. A towering monument on a nearby hill stood sentry above the city. When his leg was fully dressed, the doctor told him to lie back so he could give him something for the pain. He felt the needle pierce his skin. It was not long before drowsiness overcame him.

He woke up early fully refreshed and ate a light breakfast of tea, toast and a thick gruel that stuck like glue to the side of the bowl. Despite its appearance, it was not altogether unpleasant. After breakfast, two armed guards entered his room and escorted him downstairs to a waiting ambulance. The ambulance, its sirens blaring, sped away from the spot where Mary, Queen of Scots had suffered her final defeat in 1568, and raced down Argyle Street. Hess, seated in the rear of the vehicle with the guards eyeing him cautiously from the opposite bench, attempted to make conversation. They looked away, embarrassed.

The weather had turned nasty overnight. A steady downpour washed the grime along the sidewalks in swirling gray streams. The speeding ambulance continued up Maryhill Road past gray stone buildings through the gritty working-class corner of Glasgow that had been pounded severely by German bombs. Hess noted the rubble piled beside the road, the jagged walls of bombed-out apartment buildings that had once housed the city's poor.

The Maryhill Barracks were a series of red stone buildings built over 200 years earlier in an area now contained by the sprawling slums of Glasgow. Hess limped noticeably down the ambulance ramp, assisted by a medic with a Red Cross patch on his arm. The ankle was starting to hurt badly for the first time. When he saw where he was, he looked around wildly—this was not what he had expected. Why was he here at this squalid army barracks instead of at the Duke of Hamilton's estate?

It wasn't as if his journey had been arranged without the duke's full knowledge and cooperation. Of course, his fiery arrival had not been part of the plan. Because of it, he had engendered unwanted publicity. He must keep the press from discovering who he was. Surely, his friend the Duke of Hamilton would not want his identity made public either. It was absolutely urgent that he speak to the duke at once, before somebody recognized him, and have him deliver Hess's message to Churchill as soon as possible. If Churchill were at all interested in his proposal for Operation Barbarossa, he would most likely want to coordinate his own cover story with the Führer's.

Hess trembled. Hitler would be furious about the way things were developing. The entire idea for the mission had been his own, and it was his responsibility to make sure he carried it out successfully. Now this crash landing in Scotland would cause embarrassment for everyone. Would his wife be safe? His adjutant? Hitler would possibly want to implement his contingency plan—the story of Hess's insanity—to forestall any future problems if Hess's identity were made known. Better to put the matter out in the open now than to be embarrassed with it later on. How much time did he have? A day or two at most. He had to speak to Hamilton, and have Hamilton communicate his message to Churchill at once.

His new room was smaller than the first one, little more than a cell. A uniformed man with a ludicrous accent burst in and identified himself as a captain of the Scottish Guards.

"Your name, please," he said.

"I am Captain Alfred Horn of the Luftwaffe. Captain Alfred . . .

"I haird you. What are you doing in Scotland, Captain Horn?"

"I have come on a mission of peace."

"You speak English quite well."

Hess did not reply.

"Peace, you say? Your plane could hardly have held enough petrol for the flight from Germany, let alone for a retairn journey."

"Sir, I am here on a top-secret mission. I have information for the Duke of Hamilton. I must speak to him at once."

"Personal friend of yours, is he?"

Hess stared at his interrogator.

"He knows I'm here, Captain. If you will only talk to him, you'll see it as exactly as I say."

Hess continued to look at the Scottish officer, smiling a smile that never reached his eyes. That was the way the Führer smiled, but Hess's version didn't have the same effect. When Hitler did it, people trembled. Not this Scotsman. He merely stared back at Hess with a derisive grin of his own. Hess held his gaze as long as he could, then was forced to look away.

The officer withdrew from the room, leaving Hess alone with two armed guards at the door. The German's face was burning. Somehow, he would find a way to assert his authority. Outside in the hallway he could hear muffled voices, but not what was being said. He sensed that his request—his demand—was being discussed. After an absence of perhaps fifteen minutes, the captain of the Scottish Guards returned.

"I've just been on the wire with the Duke of Hamilton," he said.

"Yes?"

"He has no knowledge of a Captain Horn or any secret mission."

"But that . . . you see . . ."

"He ordered that you be detained as a prisoner of war."

"But surely he . . . he can't just leave it at that. He must wish to investigate this matter himself. Yes?"

"The duke will be here shortly," the Scotsman said. "He will continue with the interrogation. That is all for now."
He turned and left the room.

THE DUKE OF Hamilton, last in line of a family that had received its title from James II of Scotland 500 years before, was not looking forward to this meeting. A lean, pleasant-looking man of medium height, he was being whisked by his driver along the Eaglesham Road from his estate toward the heart of Glasgow. Of all the monumental blunders, this one was without equal. Captain Alfred Horn indeed! How long could the deception last—hours? days?—before somebody recognized the bloody fool? The Deputy Führer of all the Nazis! Good Lord! What could he do to salvage the situation?

Hamilton went directly to Hess's room, where he was greeted by the captain who had conducted the initial inter-rogation.

"Sorry to roust you oot this early, sir," he said. "But our errant Nazi here insisted on speaking to you directly. I thought perhaps you might have better luck with him than I."

"No trouble, Captain. You did the proper thing. I . . . I'd like a word with him alone."

"Really, sir? Do you think you'll be safe, sir?"

"He's hardly in a condition to pose any threat. Post your guards in the hallway outside and give me twenty minutes."

"Very good, sir." The officer saluted smartly and left the room.

Hess had been sitting in a chair staring intently at Hamilton throughout this exchange. Once they were alone he made an effort to rise, but Hamilton motioned for him to remain seated. The duke recognized at once the stern visage and bushy eyebrows of the man he had met at the Olympic Games in Berlin five years before. That curious face. Long, thin.

Those wet eyes that belonged more to a suffering artist than to a top-ranking Nazi. Hamilton had been struck by him the first time they met. Such a study in contradictions.

"You were expecting me," said Hess.

"I was expecting no one," Hamilton said.

"But surely you received the message concerning my mission."

"I received nothing from you or anyone else in Germany, do you understand?"

"But you responded favorably to Herr Professor Haushofer. You . . ."

"Listen to me! All of this must be denied. This situation you've created here is impossible."

"Yes, yes, I understand. Unfortunately, my accident has complicated things. But the future of the war and the safety of your country depend on the success of my mission."

Hamilton blanched. How could he make this man understand his position? British intelligence had questioned him about the message that they had intercepted from his Nazi contacts. He had claimed, of course, he knew nothing—he was not in communication with Nazi officials, the entire business was apparently a diversionary tactic to confuse and divide their enemies.

"This continual fighting between England and Germany is not in the interests of either country," Hess said. "Stalin is waiting for us to bleed each other to death so he can emerge as the true victor in this conflict. Churchill must be made to see this clearly. All we ask is that he leave us alone until we complete the job of ridding the world of Bolshevism."

"My dear fellow, your Fifth Column has failed to sway British public opinion. The English people remain firmly committed to the war against fascism. We cannot proceed any further. We've reached an impasse."

"The English people! Who are the English people? Aren't

you representative of the English people too? Surely others will listen when they understand that Germany has no claims on English territories. Opening a second front at this stage of the war is futile."

Hamilton sighed. They had been through all of it before. The man in front of him, so reasonable when last they met, looked at him with a fanatical intensity that made Hamilton acutely uncomfortable.

"Listen to me, Hess," Hamilton said. "The entire country will be demanding to know how a German pilot was able to penetrate our air defenses and parachute safely onto Scottish soil. There will be an investigation. A scapegoat must be found, and I very much suspect it could be me since this is my bailiwick up here. Alfred Horn indeed! How long do you think we can perpetrate that deception? Whatever chance your mission had of succeeding was destroyed along with your aircraft. We must abort it and come up with some sort of plausible explanation for your presence here."

"The Führer already has such an explanation prepared. I believe he could be preparing to release it already."

"What sort of explanation?"

"Please. We have so little time. You will be conferring with your prime minister about this?"

"Of course. As I said, this is my watch you've blundered in on. God only knows what I'm going to say to him."

"Just deliver my message then, without implicating yourself. Tell him Rudolf Hess took it upon himself to fly to England and plead Germany's cause. It is the truth after all, is it not?"

Hamilton could not help smiling despite his predicament. "I must say, sometimes the easiest approach is also the most obvious. Why not indeed?"

"It is always the best not to stray too far from the truth. Selective truth, if you prefer."

"I'm flying down to London this afternoon to report to Winston," Hamilton said. "He won't have much time to make a decision, not with every journalist and reporter in the country—in the world, I daresay—clamoring for a story."

"What is to become of me in the meanwhile?" Hess asked.

"I'll have you taken to more secure quarters, where you'll be kept in isolation. You'll find the captain's room more comfortable, and it's easier to isolate you there until we figure out what to do."

"I assume I'll be permitted to return to Germany through a neutral country regardless of the success or failure of my mission?"

Hamilton stared at him for a long moment. That was impossible, no matter what the outcome of his meeting with the prime minister. To allow a top-ranking enemy officer to go free in the midst of a war—whether there was to be a degree of cooperation between the warring powers or not—was unthinkable.

"Of course," Hamilton said. "I'll discuss it with Churchill when I see him."

WHEN HAMILTON LEFT the building minutes later, he was dismayed to see a gaggle of reporters straining to get through to him from behind a cordon of military police. It would be difficult, to say the least, to keep Hess's identity secret much longer—particularly if someone were to get a good look at him. Photographs of Hitler and his top-ranking officers had been published in all the newspapers on several occasions.

"The incident is being investigated," he said in a response to a barrage of shouted questions. Within moments his motorcar was inching its way through the impatient crowd, parting the sea of bellowing humanity as it carried him to Paisley Airdrome.

CHAPTER FIVE

ORDINARILY, HAMILTON WOULD have enjoyed the drive out to Woodstock, the small village south of Blenheim Castle where Churchill had been born. Certainly, the weather in England was a marked improvement over the cold, damp grip of lingering winter he had left behind in Scotland. Early signs of spring were visible everywhere, moving the English countryside toward the vivid green lushness that would last until the first frost in the fall. But the duke had too much on his mind to concentrate on the beauty of his surroundings.

Churchill had moved there after the Nazis had tried—unsuccessfully—to bomb his house in Chequers several times. Winston was something of a fatalist, but the last round of bombs had fallen too close for comfort. The eighteenth-century mansion in Woodstock offered to him for the duration of the war suited him just fine. It was a perfect weekend retreat, an appropriate setting for private conferences such as the one Hamilton was racing to today.

Contributing to the duke's anxiety was the fact that he

didn't quite know what to expect. His tension increased as the police car barreled along thousand-year-old cobblestone streets, past shops filled with sweets and antique furniture, toward the prime minister's mansion.

When the Duke of Hamilton reached his destination, he was ushered immediately into Churchill's library. He faltered—imperceptibly, he hoped—when he discovered that the great man was not alone. The prime minister rose with surprising grace for a man of his girth and extended his right hand in greeting. His trademark Dunhill cigar, freshly lit, was firmly clenched in his left. The duke shook hands with Lord Beaverbrook, formerly Max Aitken, the Canadian-born press baron who owned the largest string of newspapers in England and Scotland. Churchill introduced him next to Sir John Simon, the lord chancellor, who was said to be the prime minister's chief adviser.

Simon, a veteran politician who had held cabinet posts in several previous administrations, was an imposing figure with an almost military bearing. He was six feet tall, bone-thin, and his high intelligence blazed out of his clear brown eyes. For some reason Hamilton's hand shook when he grasped Simon's.

The men took their seats in a semicircle of sorts around the prime minister. Hamilton was accustomed to wealth, but there was always something awe-inspiring about planting his feet on a carpet that surely cost more than most of his countrymen made in a year. His eyes quickly took in the lavish Victorian and Georgian furnishings, the heavy red leather upholstered sofas and easy chairs, the panelled walls covered with French, English, and Italian paintings, the Royal Worcester, Crown Derby and Coalport porcelains, the silver centerpiece with six silver hanging baskets placed in the middle of the coffee table. Nor did he fail to notice the well-stocked bar across the library with its decanters of amber whiskey and the dark brandy that Churchill was so fond of.

"So, James," said the prime minister, "tell us just what sort of debacle we have on our hands."

Hamilton cleared his throat. "To start with, gentlemen," he said, "you should know that Captain Alfred Horn is none other than Rudolf Hess, Deputy Führer of Germany."

"He told you this?" said Simon.

"Actually he didn't have to. I'd met him before during the 'thirty-six games in Berlin. Recognized him at once." The duke forced himself to hold John Simon's gaze without wavering.

"Go on," said Simon.

"The man's half mad. He took it upon himself to fly off on his own to see if he could change the direction of the war. According to Hess, Hitler is planning to launch a blitzkrieg on his eastern front against Russia focused primarily on Lithuania in the north and the Ukraine in the south."

Churchill stood up, hovering directly over Hamilton, a veil of smoke clouding his features.

"It can't possibly succeed," he said. "Surely Hitler knows that."

"The Germans think it can . . . under certain conditions. They have far superior forces. By transferring two hundred divisions to the eastern front, it's conceivable they could occupy Moscow, Leningrad and Stalingrad before winter. The Russians would be virtually defenseless against that kind of assault, sir."

"My dear Hamilton," Beaverbrook said, "Hitler can't possibly move all that manpower and machinery to the Russian front. He'd be leaving himself completely open on his western flank. Not even the Wehrmacht can spread itself so thin and survive."

"That's what I meant before when I said the plan could succeed . . . under certain conditions. Hess flew here to offer us a proposition. The German plan can work only if Britain agrees not to open a second front on the continent. Hess sees Bolshevism as the common enemy of both Germany and the United Kingdom. Hitler's main goal is lebensraum on the continent, living space that can only be attained by spreading toward the east. He wants the natural resources of Poland, the granaries of the Ukraine, and the oil of the Caucasus to which he feels Germany is historically entitled."

Churchill sat back down, nodded toward his chief adviser.

"Are we to believe," said Simon, "that Rudolf Hess flew here on an imbecile mission completely on his own? That he undertook such a proposterous venture without Hitler's approval?"

"As I mentioned before, I believe the man is mad. He believes fanatically in his vision of an accommodation between our countries."

"We are being asked to sit by," said Churchill, "while Hitler rids the world of Bolshevism. Is that what you're telling us?"

"That's essentially how he put it, yes. Hitler will agree to retreat from France and Holland once he's conquered Russia and resettled millions of Germans in the east. His occupation of Europe is proving too costly. Germany's historical destiny, as he sees it, is eastward expansion."

"Treachery, pure and simple," Churchill said. There was spittle on his lower lip.

"How can we be sure Hitler won't turn an acquisitive eye on us once he's accomplished his goals in Russia—with our complicity?" Simon wanted to know.

"Hess claims Hitler is quite willing to coexist freely with the British empire. Otherwise, if the war is fought to its conclusion, England and Germany will slowly destroy each other and Stalin will emerge as the only victor."

"I'm afraid this doesn't sound much like the ravings of a

mad underling to me," said Simon. "It has all the earmarks of a well-thought-out master plan straight from the brain of a sane and calculating Rudolf Hess, or quite possibly even Adolph Hitler himself. He's hell-bent on conquering the entire world."

"How did you leave it with Hess?" asked Churchill. "What sort of promises did you make?"

"Promises? None, of course. Other than that I would convey his message to you. I told him quite frankly that I regarded his proposal as out of the question."

"It's apparent to me that Hess is acting with the full authority of his Führer," Beaverbrook said.

"Hess says Great Britain can't win on her own," Hamilton said. "Our allies are defeated, our only hope is the United States—which remains reluctant to get involved. The Americans have their own problems. Germany maintains an effective Fifth Column in the States with ties to sympathetic industrialists. Besides . . . the United States will soon be occupied with a war of its own. Hess told me that Japan is preparing an attack to divert American attention toward the Pacific."

"Indeed," said Simon. He looked at the prime minister. "Just where and when is this alleged attack to take place?"

"He wouldn't be that specific. His main point was, if England is expecting America to come to its aid, we're going to be sorely disappointed."

"You've pled the enemy's cause quite well," Churchill said.

"I'm only passing on the substance of the conversation I had with Hess this morning."

"Sir John," Churchill said, his eyes fixed on Hamilton.

"You've been in contact with the Nazis for quite some time now," Simon said.

Hamilton kept his voice steady. "I'm afraid I don't know what you're referring to."

"You know very well what I'm referring to. Two letters, in particular, addressed to you from Albrecht Haushofer and sent via Mrs. Violet Roberts in Lisbon. You were, I believe, already questioned about them by intelligence."

"I was. And I'll tell you now what I told intelligence then. I never received any letters. They—"

"SIS forwarded them to you after making copies," Simon said.

"And I never—Surely you're not questioning my loyalty. This is a diversionary tactic of the Nazis—which evidently has succeeded to some degree."

Simon looked back at Churchill, still staring at Hamilton through a swirl of blue-gray smoke. There was a touch of something—whimsy? mischief? malice?—in his eyes. Whatever it was, Hamilton felt like odd man out.

"What I'm about to tell you," the prime minister said, "must be kept in the strictest confidence. We are all sworn to secrecy here. Do I have your word?"

"Without question, sir. I swear to it."

For a long moment, the only sound in the room was the ticking of the ornate clock across the room that suddenly took on a disproportionate resonance.

"The Haushofers received an answer to their letter a fortnight ago in Lisbon," Churchill said.

Hamilton remained silent.

"SIS intercepted that as well, but we decided to let it go through. You were expecting Hess all the while, James. You can't deny it."

The shock of Churchill's words sent a chill through Hamilton.

"After consulting with the people present in this room tonight," Churchill continued, "I decided to give Hess and his beloved Führer all the rope they desire. Why not allow Hitler to think that he has carte blanche to divert eighty percent of his forces to the eastern front? If he believes he has a pact with us, it gives us the flexibility we need to conduct the future of the war in any manner we choose."

Hamilton, stunned, was beyond making any response. So they knew Hess was coming all the time. They had used him, and his contact with the Germans, without him being aware of it. He was about to register a complaint, then suddenly realized he was in no position to do so. It was he, after all, who had been in communication with England's sworn enemy—an act in and of itself that could be construed by some as an act of treason. British intelligence had uncovered him weeks, perhaps months, before. He had allowed himself to be set up as the man in the middle should the whole plan come crashing down around them.

This despite the fact that he did not regard his own actions as treasonous. His prime interest all along had been his country's security. Many right-thinking Britons, including the Duke of Windsor (along with his American wife) considered Churchill's unswerving enmity toward the Germans as the surest path to self-destruction. It would result only in the final dismemberment of the entire British Empire. But how could he explain this now when Churchill and his entourage had manipulated him into a position that, on the surface, smacked of conspiring with the enemy during a time of war?

"Am I to understand, sir," Hamilton said finally, "that our plan is to make Hitler think we are receptive to his proposal?"

"We are not quite that far along as yet," the prime minister said. "Our main concern at this moment is controlling the damage caused by Hess's dramatic entry onto our shores. We didn't anticipate an arrival that would be so highly publicized."

"It's just a question of time," Beaverbrook said, "before one of my intrepid scribblers unearths the true identity of our visitor."

"Perhaps we should issue a statement now to avoid any semblance of duplicity," said Simon.

"Better we let Hitler offer his own explanation first," Churchill said. "I've already instructed Lord Halifax to contact the German embassy in Dublin and coordinate it."

"In the meantime," said Simon, "we've got to remove Hess from his present quarters before Glasgow is swarming with correspondents."

"I have a plan," the prime minister said. "Take the train to Glasgow this evening, Sir John, and speak to Hess yourself. Assure him that his proposal has been well received, that we're considering the matter. We'll fit him out in civilian clothes and put his uniform on one of our German prisoners who matches up passably well to his appearance.

"The real Hess will be transported to a destination I already have in mind—isolated from the press—while his double will be publicly displayed in the Tower of London. I don't want the real Hess there, with reporters from all over the world hanging about, ready to swarm all over him. The double will serve as a lightning rod for the storm that's sure to break as soon as the public finds out who he is."

"That's awfully risky," said Simon.

"Not nearly so risky as letting Hitler know where his real Deputy Führer is being housed. It's not beyond him to attempt to bomb Hess into oblivion now that he's delivered his message. That's one more reason I want a double there. If the Luftwaffe succeeds in obliterating London Tower with him in it, the world will forget all about Rudolf Hess rather quickly."

Churchill looked from Simon to Hamilton, then back at Simon.

"One more thing," he said.

"Yes?" said Simon.

"Don't let Hess know you're Jewish. Use your alias when you meet him."

The Duke of Hamilton suddenly knew why he feared Sir John Simon the moment he entered the room. The man detested him because of his attitude toward the Germans—even before they met.

"As for you, my dear Hamilton," Churchill said, "I think it's best if you have no further contact with our celebrated guest . . . or any of his compatriots. I think you're well aware of your situation here."

CHAPTER SIX

THE YOUNG-LOOKING reporter with the sandy hair watched his breath fog the air as he waited for the Duke of Hamilton to emerge from Maryhill Barracks following his interview with the German pilot. The weather was raw, and the reporters who were cordoned off behind the line of military police hunched their shoulders in a futile attempt to ward off the cold. The duke had been inside for some time now, and the man and his colleagues were anxious to get some information about the German who had crash-landed on Scottish soil.

Finally, Hamilton emerged, his stern face partially in shadow beneath the visor of his cap. He carried his heavy wool overcoat casually over his left forearm, which left the eagle and rows of ribbons sewn above the left breast pocket of his uniform clearly visible. The duke scarcely acknowledged their presence as he mumbled unintelligibly before disappearing inside his waiting motorcar.

The reporter was furious. Clearly, something hush-hush

was going on, and if there was one thing that drove Philip Renfield crazy it was being kept in the dark. Lord knows, his profession was a low-paying one, but he had felt called to it from the time he was a kid. There had never been any question in his mind that he was here on earth to search out the truth and set it down in writing.

Despite his youthful appearance, Philip was closing in fast on his thirty-seventh birthday. Up close, the worry lines and crevices were visible in his face, particularly when he was nursing a hangover—as was the case this morning. He had been knocking back a pint of bitters, perhaps his sixth of the evening, when the news swept through the barroom like a contagion. A downed aircraft. German. Crashed in flames on a farm outside the city. The story took on new facets each time a new link in the gossip chain passed it along.

This was the sort of thing that sustained him. He had married the daughter of Michael Chandler Buchanan, the owner of the newspaper he worked for, and risen from copy boy to star reporter during the past decade. But that was due more to his hard work in pursuit of a story than to his serendipitous marriage—a marriage that was all but over. Damn Susan anyway! He was in his mid-twenties when they met and she was barely out of her teens. It was a mismatch from the start. Susan preferred the comforts of home—which she thought included an attentive husband. He was married to his job. It was something of a miracle that Susan had stuck it out for nearly a decade before leaving him to pursue a career of her own in London.

But still he got on well with old man Buchanan, who treated him more like the son he never had than like a son-in-law— despite the failure of the marriage. Philip worked harder than most of his colleagues, and his father-in-law rewarded him for his efforts. He dug hard and deep until he was convinced he had uncovered the facts. Even last night, half drunk as he was, he had raced out into the night looking for the spot where the German plane came down.

He coughed loudly. His winter cold, aggravated by too many cigarettes, refused to go away. Already he had wasted too much time this morning. He felt obliged to be on hand outside Maryhill with the rest of the press corps just in case something developed. It would not do to miss it. But at the moment he was chilled to the bone, not to mention his throbbing head and churning stomach, and—as he expected—his vigil had been in vain. Of course the duke had nothing to say. Of course there would be nothing forthcoming from official sources until they all conferred in London with Winston and cleared it with the great man first. It was time to do what all good reporters have to do if they want to get the scoop on a story: He had to play inspector and dig a little deeper beneath the surface. It would pay to keep a close watch on Maryhill Barracks and see what developed. The real story was hidden there inside, not in the official blather that would be forthcoming from London.

PHILIP WAITED OUTSIDE for a long while after the other reporters had dispersed, but it was clear that nothing new was going to take place until Hamilton received his orders from Churchill. He returned to Maryhill early the next morning, and was quickly joined by an impatient crowd of his fellow news hounds. At 10:37 in the morning, the front gate of Maryhill Barracks swung open.

The prisoner—tall, gaunt, dressed in his Luftwaffe uniform—limped down the steps between two rows of military police. The gaggle of reporters strained forward, screaming for information about the Nazi.

"Where are you taking him?"

"How did he get through our bloody defenses?"

"Was he alone?"

"How many others got through with him?"

The reporters' questions hung in the air, unanswered.

The guards helped the prisoner into the rear of a military truck. The captain of the Scottish Guards who had first interrogated Hess approached the crowd of reporters and raised his hands for silence.

"I've been informed," he said, "that the prisoner will be taken to London for questioning. The entire incident is being investigated. You'll have the answers to your questions just as soon as they're available."

"Why was he alone? It doesn't make any sense."

"That's all I have for now. Sorry. I understand the government will be issuing a statement shortly."

The young captain turned on his heel and disappeared back into the barracks, ignoring their clamor for additional information. Finally, realizing that this was all they were going to get from him today, the reporters scurried to find the nearest telephones and report their meager findings to their news desks. Within moments they were scattered like so many motes of dust in the wind, except for a lone correspondent who hung in the background.

Philip Renfield crossed the street and entered the warm interior of a tea shop. He took a table near the window facing onto the pavement, where he could see clearly the entrance to the barracks across the way. The warm air tingled his face, reddened his cheeks. His nostrils flared and he breathed in the damp aroma of brewing tea and assorted sweets. Something about this entire affair did not sit well with him. He couldn't quite put his finger on it, but a sixth sense that he had developed throughout his years as a reporter told him to hang around a bit longer instead of following the herd in its race to file a story with no meat on it.

Thirty-seven minutes later, Philip Renfield's patience was rewarded. A new phalanx of military police emerged from Maryhill Barracks with a man in civilian dress closely under guard. They walked across the now-deserted pavement, the civilian limping badly. The guards herded their prisoner into the back of a large olive-green lorry similar to the one that had been waiting for the first prisoner. This man was tall and thin, with dark hair and thick, bushy eyebrows shadowing his face.

Philip could not be certain, but it seemed to him that he had seen that face before. It was distinctive, somewhat unusual in its intensity. It was not a face that one forgot easily. Something about the look of almost fanatical devotion in the eyes. And why had two men been led from Maryhill Barracks under guard? Clearly, something was going on that the government did not want the public to know about. His curiosity aroused to begin with, Philip was completely alert now. He was determined to find out what was going on—if it was the last thing he did.

CHAPTER SEVEN

PHILIP RENFIELD RUSHED from the small shop and hopped on his battered motorbike. Keeping a safe distance behind he trailed the lorry to a small suburb of Glasgow, where it entered the drive of a secluded estate. Again, Philip saw the man, whose distinctive features struck a chord, as he limped from the lorry to the doorway of the house.

PHILIP RACED BACK to his office as fast as he could. When he arrived, he dug through the files until he collected all the photographs he thought he would need. Then he ran back outside and got on his bike without bothering to respond to his editor's query as to where he was flying off to in such a hurry. With the wind tearing at his clothes and hair, he swept up Eaglesham Road as fast as his sputtering machine could carry him. The ride seemed interminable, but fortunately for him the traffic was light and he soon reached the open fields and hedgerows that marked his destination. An elderly woman opened the door after his second knock.

"I'm Philip Renfield from the *Daily Record*," he said. "I'm looking for Mr. McLean."

"Aye, you and half of Scotland," she said. "My son hasn't had a moment to hi'self since the other evening."

"It's important. I . . . I have something to show him that might help everyone learn the truth. May I speak with him for just a moment?"

"Who is it now?" Philip heard the voice call from inside the cottage.

"A newspaperman from the *Daily Record*. Says he has something he'd like to show you."

"Invite him in, then. We'll all catch our death with the door open."

The kitchen was warm and snug, with a fire burning in the hearth. Philip introduced himself to the farmer and asked him if he was the man who had found the fallen German the night before.

"Aye, and I wish he'd landed somewhere else. He found me is more like it. I brought him in and sat him down right there in front of the fire while I called the local gairds."

"Did he identify himself?"

"Said he was a captain or something in the German air division. Alfred Horn, I believe. Demanded to speak to the duke himself and was quite cheeky about it."

"What did he look like? Any distinguishing characteristics?"

"Quite distinctive, he was. A tall fellow, thin, with a bushy thatch unlike any I've ever seen for eyebrows."

Philip Renfield opened the envelope he had taken from his office, pulled out a sheaf of photographs and spread them out on the farmer's table—the grainy likenesses of top Nazis, including Hitler, that the newspaper kept on file.

"Can you recognize Alfred Horn in any of these pictures?"

David McLean studied them intently for several moments, then leaned forward and tapped the second one from the left with his finger. It was a photograph of Rudolf Hess.

"That's him. No question about it."

"Are you absolutely sure?"

"Beyond a doubt."

SIR JOHN SIMON descended from the train onto the platform in Glasgow. His worst fears were confirmed immediately. Scarcely had the soles of his hand-sewn English brogans touched the pavement than a paperboy hawking the evening edition of the *Daily Record* caught his attention. He quickened his pace along the platform and gave the boy a copper coin. The headline assaulted him like a slap on his face:

RUDOLF HESS IN GLASGOW

Sir John quickly scanned the subhead and the first paragraph of the story, which ran without benefit of a byline:

HERR HESS, HITLER'S RIGHT-HAND MAN, HAS RUN AWAY FROM GERMANY AND IS IN GLASGOW SUFFERING FROM A BROKEN ANKLE.
Rudolf Hess, Deputy Führer of Germany and party leader of the National Socialist Party, has landed in Scotland. . . .

A side story to the left of the main article presented the farmer's account of the incident in his own words:

I FOUND GERMAN LYING IN FIELD
David McLean, a plowman, was the man who found Rudolf Hess. Here is McLean's own story as told to the *Daily Record*, the first newspaper on the scene:

"I was in the house and everyone else was in bed late at night when I heard the plane roaring overhead. As I ran out to the back of the farm I heard a crash, and saw the plane burst into flames in a field about 200 yards away.

"I was amazed and a bit frightened when I saw a parachute dropping slowly through the gathering darkness . . ."

Simon did not have to read further to understand that a change of plans was in order. First, he had to get on the phone to London and speak to Churchill at once. There was no question but that the government would have to issue a statement immediately confirming the story, or run the risk of appearing to be hiding something. Damn that reporter, whoever he was! By breaking the story before clearing it with London, he had made the government look like a pack of fools at best, conspiratorial at worst.

Next, he would have to remove Hess from Glasgow at the earliest opportunity and put him in hiding, as far away as possible from snooping correspondents. Churchill's Tower of London plan, which he personally considered a bit daffy, would have to be set in motion right away—without further discussion. The entire world would demand a more detailed explanation as to exactly what Hess was doing here. He would have to coordinate everything with Halifax in Dublin. There was no time left.

THE FIRST RESULTS of Simon's helter-skelter activity were in evidence the following morning. The *Daily Record* carried a follow-up story to its scoop of the previous evening. This one fairly glowed with self-satisfaction:

An official statement issued from 10 Downing Street at 11:20 last night said, "On the night of Saturday the 10th, a Messerschmitt 110 was reported by war patrols to have crossed the coast of Scotland and be flying in the direction of Glasgow. Since a Messerschmitt 110 would not have the fuel to return to Germany, this report was at first disbelieved.

"The pilot of the aircraft has been positively identified as . . ."

Overnight, Sir John Simon had turned his suite of rooms at the Central Station Hotel—the old Victorian structure built inside the terminal—into a veritable command post. His entourage occupied other rooms on the same floor on either side of his own.

He had traveled to Scotland and checked into the hotel under the name of "Dr. Guthrie," not only to hide his Jewish heritage from Hess but also to keep the press off his scent. It would be difficult enough getting the real Hess to a safe house and his double publicly transported into the Tower of London without unnecessary complications.

Simon picked up his bedside phone, then placed it back on its cradle. He would call the prime minister again later, after he spoke to Herr Deputy Führer Rudolf Hess.

CHAPTER EIGHT

THE DUKE OF Hamilton was waiting in his blue Jaguar on the corner of Argyle Street. Sir John Simon slid quickly into the front passenger seat, his aide into the rear.

"Where are we going, Sir John?" Hamilton said.

"Doctor Guthrie," Simon said. "You might as well get in the habit of calling me that before we meet with Herr Hess."

Simon gave directions to a location in the Pollockshields section of Glasgow, a suburb characterized by huge red stone houses on two-acre sites.

"Is this where he's to be housed, then?" asked Hamilton.

"Temporarily. After our meeting today he'll be transferred to Abergavenny in South Wales. There's an estate there surrounded by two hundred acres of deserted woodlands. With half the world's attention focused on the Tower of London, we'll have at least reasonable assurance that the newspaper bloodhounds will be kept off his trail."

"As far as today's meeting is concerned, I understand . . ."

"Your role will be confined to introducing me to Hess—as

Doctor Guthrie, special aide to the prime minister—then taking your leave to attend an urgent meeting. He trusts you, it seems. Once that confidence is transferred to me, I'll handle the rest."

Hamilton fumed. He didn't enjoy being relegated to the role of batman after setting up the most critical liaison of the war, one that would divert England away from this senseless conflict with Germany and save the empire from extinction. Once Windsor was restored to the throne, he wouldn't have to put up any longer with people like John Simon.

They drove in silence up the long curving driveway and stopped in front of a red stone mansion covered with snaking vines. Two burly men in civilian clothes, assigned by Scotland Yard, received the party of three and ushered them inside. There was a broad staircase to the left of the entrance hall that ascended to the upstairs bedrooms, and a living room as large as a ballroom off to the right with an old Georgian coal-burning fireplace providing the only heat.

RUDOLF HESS, WHO had been sitting in front of the glowing coals alone with his thoughts, rose anxiously when he saw the Duke of Hamilton approaching him from the entrance hall. Hamilton smiled and extended his right hand in greeting.

"You have been treated well these last few days?"

"Yes, yes. You have news for me?"

"I would like you to meet Doctor Guthrie, special aide to Prime Minister Churchill."

Hess clicked his heels smartly and flashed a smile.

"I am honored," he said.

"The honor is mine," Simon said. He smiled broadly at the Deputy Führer of the Third Reich and even managed to inject a tinge of warmth into his eyes. *So this was what one of the chief architects of the most brutal dictatorship of modern times looked like up close. Human, like everyone else.* The realization chilled Simon's heart.

"You have my absolute assurance," Hamilton said, "that Doctor Guthrie speaks directly for the prime minister. It is as though Winston Churchill himself were here."

Hess clicked his heels again and bowed slightly in Simon's direction.

"I must leave now on some urgent business," Hamilton said. "But Doctor Guthrie will see to it that you are housed in more comfortable surroundings after today."

"Perhaps some tea first," said Simon after Hamilton left. "And then we can get down to the matter at hand. I've taken the liberty of bringing an interpreter with me in case you find it more convenient to express yourself in German."

"English is fine," said Hess, "but I thank you for the gesture."

Simon nodded and the interpreter left the room. A servant entered with a silver tea service and a tray of pastries, then withdrew and left the two men to themselves. For a long moment the soft hissing from the glowing coals was the only sound in the cavernous room.

"The duke has conveyed your message to the prime minister and me," Simon said finally. "Your proposal is under serious consideration."

"Churchill is favorably disposed, then?" Hess arched the thatch of brow that ran thickly across his lower forehead. The recalcitrant Churchill was considered the major stumbling block in Hitler's plan. The bulldog had objected to the Duke of Windsor's overtures to Germany at every turn and was known to be bitterly opposed to Germany's claims on the eastern lands.

"Make no mistake about it," Simon said. "The prime minister has no sympathy for the tenets of National Socialism, any more than he does for those of Bolshevism. Whatever deci-

sion he makes will be for purely tactical reasons. He's aware—quite aware—that without American support, the best England can hope for in this struggle is a stalemate. Your proposal interests us only because an understanding with Germany may be the only way to keep our empire intact."

"Many highly respected Britons are sympathetic to our cause," said Hess. "They understand that international Bolshevism is a greater threat to England's security than Germany is. Once Germany has achieved its goal for eastward expansion and fulfilled its historical destiny, the Third Reich will be content to share world power with a strong and unified England."

"We're aware of these sympathizers you speak of. Oswald Mosley and his Fascist band . . ."

"Beyond Mosley. I am referring to respected members of the royal family, leading politicians and military officers. Only Churchill stands in the way of a mutually acceptable agreement that will benefit both our countries."

"Perhaps. Until now he's been counting on American support in coming to the aid of France and western Europe. But you told Hamilton the United States will soon be preoccupied with problems of its own in the Pacific."

Hess picked up his teacup and sipped slowly before replacing it in the tray. He looked directly at Simon and measured his words carefully.

"We have known for quite some time that England has not the military strength to rescue France. Hitler's generals, and Göring in particular, have been imploring the Führer to unleash a storm of wrath and steel upon your country. The Luftwaffe is in full readiness and awaits the Führer's word. But he has resisted—only because he feels it is still possible to reach an agreement with England that will make further bloodshed unnecessary. Once Churchill understands that no help will be forthcoming from the Americans, Hitler is certain

that reason will prevail and Churchill will be compelled to make the only correct decision. That is why I am here. I represent England's last opportunity to avoid total extinction."

Simon remained silent for nearly a minute. He knew precisely when the critical moment had arrived in any negotiation. The next words uttered could well determine the future direction of the war.

"When will Japan's attack on the United States take place?"

"Soon. The exact time has not yet been determined."

"Has the precise target been selected?"

"Yes, but I am not at liberty to say what it is."

"I see. If your military operation against Russia were to go forward, are you absolutely certain you've not underestimated Russian strength?"

"Operation Barbarossa has been planned with utmost thoroughness. There is no chance of the Wehrmacht failing in its objective. Our blitzkrieg will be over in a matter of months. Once England gives us a free hand we are prepared to turn our attention toward the east and guarantee the continuation of your empire."

"How soon can Barbarossa be initiated?"

"Within a month of reaching an agreement with Churchill, we will transfer two hundred divisions to the eastern front. Already aircraft are being moved into place."

"Napoleon was able to penetrate all the way to Moscow and still could not defeat the Russians."

"Napoleon didn't have five thousand tanks at his disposal, or the Luftwaffe. We are not going to repeat Napoleon's mistakes, I assure you."

"What guarantee does England have," Simon said, "that Germany will withdraw from France once you've achieved your goals in the east? And, beyond that, how can we be sure England will be left in peace?"

"Once we have annexed Poland and part of Russia into a greater Germany, we will no longer have any need for the western territories. Germany will be able to supply itself with all the grain and oil it requires, as well as land much needed for millions of our people. Hitler has always maintained that Germany's historical destiny lies to the east. He stated this unequivocally in *Mein Kampf.*"

Simon looked directly at Hess. His gaze was firm, unwavering, as was the Deputy Führer's.

"And if England refuses to go along with Hitler's plan for eastward expansion? If we refuse to cooperate with Operation Barbarossa? Then what?"

Hess seemed to have been expecting this question.

"That, my dear Doctor Guthrie, would be a most unfortunate decision for both our countries. If that were to be Churchill's final decision, then the Führer would have no choice but to accede to the wishes of Göring and his generals. The full wrath of the Third Reich would be unleashed by air and sea and land against your shores. An opportunity of great historical significance would have been lost. At worst—for you—England would be destroyed in a fortnight. At best, our countries would decimate one another while Stalin waited patiently before moving the red armies into Europe . . . and eventually the United Kingdom."

Simon stood up and walked over to face the fiery coals glowing red in the old Georgian fireplace. He spoke softly into the fire, his words carrying the weight that only war, bloodshed and the unspeakable burden of a million anguished souls could give them.

"Germany has broken every agreement it's made with every country it dealt with over the decades. And now you are asking us to believe that Hitler will not break this one. Still . . . I don't see what other choice I have. Tomorrow I will meet with Prime Minister Churchill to report on our meeting. I intend to recommend that he accept your proposal."

Hess's face fairly blazed with excitement. He started to move toward Simon, his hand outstretched, but the implacable contempt in Simon's eyes stopped him cold.

"I have nothing further to say on the subject now," Simon said. "You'll be transferred to an estate in South Wales, where you will be housed in comfort surrounded by two hundred acres of woodlands. Our next meeting will take place there within forty-eight hours, I should think. I'll give you the prime minister's decision at that time."

Simon shouldered his burden, wheeled about abruptly, and strode from the room.

CHAPTER NINE

GERMANS AND BRITISH BOTH CLAIM HESS MAD

Hitler's Right-Hand Man in Tower of London

PHILIP RENFIELD SCANNED the headline in the *Times* as he sipped his morning tea. The story in England's premier newspaper did not jibe with the facts as he knew them. The man who had been led away from Maryhill Barracks in uniform and taken to the Tower of London was not Rudolf Hess. Where was the real Hess? That was the critical question. Yet there was little he could do at the moment to overcome his frustration. When he'd filed his own story the previous afternoon with the *Daily Record*, his editor had told him in no uncertain terms that there was a hold on all features dealing with the Hess affair for reasons having to do with national security. Who had ordered the hold?

None other than old man Buchanan, his father-in-law and publisher. Certain press restrictions during wartime common in most countries were unacceptable in a democracy, Philip believed, except in matters dealing with the defense of the nation. The story he filed after tailing the lorry carrying the real Rudolf Hess to the house in Pollockshields did not fit into that category.

Unless some master deception was being perpetrated at the highest levels of the British government, a deception having to do with switched identities and a cover-up involving this Hess affair, the true meaning of which he could scarcely begin to guess. All he knew for certain was what he had seen: A man identified as Rudolf Hess led away in a van and taken to the Tower of London, where he was put on public display; another man, whom Philip was convinced was the real Nazi official, driven to a house in the suburbs of Glasgow.

What could it possibly mean?

Philip Renfield did not have the vaguest idea as yet. He merely wanted his newspaper to print the facts he had garnered to date, and he had been turned down flat. The fact that this directive had come all the way down from Buchanan spoke of hush-hush maneuverings behind the scenes, manipulations Churchill did not want the public made aware of. Despite his breakup with Susan, he was still on good terms with his father-in-law; he would have to speak with him privately about the matter. What these machinations might be he could only try to guess.

All Philip knew for sure was that a major story was unfolding, a story he meant to get to the bottom of.

SIR JOHN SIMON was uncharacteristically tense. Normally the very model of the proper British diplomat, a study in aplomb, he had difficulty containing his anxiety as he prepared for his meeting with the prime minister. So many loose ends, so many things to worry about.

First off, there was the big picture. Britain was fighting a defensive battle at the moment. Germany had subjugated

France with a minimum of effort, and the power of Hitler's Wehrmacht was all but invincible. England's very survival was at stake, the future of the empire tottering on the edge of destruction. It was impossible to see how England could withstand an onslaught of the ferocity Hess described and save itself from defeat.

Only the entry of the United States into the war could save England. Yet not only was Roosevelt dragging his feet while the future of England hung in the balance, he was demanding cash payments for needed weapons and threatening to withhold further shipments until the crown brought its accounts up to date. Isolationist sentiment ran high in America, Simon knew, and it was strengthened by the support of such powerful and influential figures as Ambassador Joseph Kennedy, industrialist Henry Ford and the popular folk hero Charles Lindbergh. Each of them had been decorated by the Führer and had visited Germany on several occasions before the war. Only a direct threat to American security itself seemed capable of swaying Roosevelt to the allied effort. An attack by Japan could be just what the situation demanded. True, it would divert America's attention toward the Pacific rim, but at least it would be a clear signal to everyone that America was as vulnerable as Europe was to the Axis menace.

Simon scribbled hurriedly on his notepad, organizing his thoughts. The immediate problem was time. Time was running out for England and western Europe. England could not afford the luxury of waiting for Japan to shake up American complacency and jolt Roosevelt into action. Churchill had been aware for some time now of the Duke of Hamilton's German sympathies, as well as the Duke of Windsor's public murmurings in support of the Nazi cause. Windsor in particular had been an embarrassment during his wanderings in Portugal and Spain. His activities and contact with leading Nazis, including Ribbentrop, Schellenberg, Heydrich and

Hess himself, had bordered on treason—even crossed the divide, many thought. Churchill had been driven into a frenzy by the duke and would have taken decisive action against him were it not for the embarrassment it would have brought the royal family.

Simon could feel his emotions quieting down as he committed his thoughts to writing. The contacts the two dukes had established had come full circle in a way impossible to predict a year earlier. Here was Hess, literally on England's doorstep, offering a proposal that would have been considered preposterous before today. Now circumstances had lent it credibility. America had not supplied the anticipated support that Churchill sought. It seemed more and more likely that Hess's proposal was the only remaining solution for England's dilemma.

Yes indeed, Simon thought. He felt much better now as he prepared to meet the prime minister.

"THIS RENFIELD CHAP bears close watching," Churchill said. The candlelight danced in his eyes, and his cheeks were flushed from the roaring fire across the room.

"I've already taken care of that," said John Simon. He was exhausted after the long train ride down from Glasgow—his second in as many days—and it showed in his lined face. "I've put two good men from SIS on the case already. He'll be kept under constant surveillance."

"We've closed the newspapers off to him, but we don't want him mouthing off to foreign correspondents. He's a loose cannon, I'm afraid."

"I agree," Simon said. "Perhaps we should confront him directly. Fire a warning shot across his bow, so to speak."

"Go ahead, then. Meanwhile, we can't keep that double in London Tower indefinitely. Should word get out that he's not

Hess, it will be all over for us. I shudder to think of the consequences if Stalin thought we were giving Hitler a hand in attacking his country."

Sir John Simon reflected on this for several moments, then carefully chose his next words.

"There may be a way to avert that possibility."

"How?"

"Suppose we send Cripps to Moscow now, to inform Stalin that Hitler will most definitely launch an attack once he's certain that Britain is destroyed."

He was referring to Sir Stafford Cripps, Great Britain's ambassador to the Soviet Union.

Churchill smiled, understanding where Simon was headed, and took a sip from his half-filled brandy snifter.

"Go on."

"He'll be indebted to us for giving him due warning—and he won't be prepared for an earlier attack by Hitler, before England falls. It will look as though Hitler changed his mind and decided to attack Russia first before attending to us."

Churchill's smile broadened. John Simon's gift for deception never failed to titillate him.

"I like it," the prime minister said, his face glowing. "I think it can work. In fact, it may well be the only plan that can. At all costs, Stalin must be kept from suspecting any accommodation between us and Hitler."

"Perhaps," said Simon, "we can induce Stalin to come to our assistance and leave himself even more vulnerable to Hitler's forces."

"Not likely," Churchill said. "He has no more concern for England's survival than for Germany's. Perhaps less. I wouldn't put it past the old devil to send word to Hitler that England is looking for his assistance, and then, when Germany's pounding us, to launch a sneak attack of his own on her eastern flank."

"Meanwhile, we have Hess to deal with," Simon said. "The wireless did report that Hitler announced he'd have him shot if he returns to Germany."

"He's living up to the legend, isn't he? He might do it just to keep up appearances."

"The public is getting hungrier by the minute for more news on the Hess affair. Glasgow hasn't received this much attention since James the Sixth took the throne."

"How we deal with Hess publicly from this moment on," Churchill said, "is critical. This insanity cover is well and good, as far as it goes. In a way it defuses some of the pressure that will be put on us to use him for propaganda."

"Quite so," said Simon. "But the press will only swallow the story for so long. Eventually, they'll want to get at him themselves. How did a madman plan a trip like this so carefully, manage to elude our border patrol and slip through to Glasgow? Why was his aircraft outfitted with such precision? Why did he demand to speak to the Duke of Hamilton after landing? All these questions and more they'll want answers to. And they'll want to get the answers directly from Hess, to judge for themselves just how crazy he is."

"Well, John." Churchill stared at the glowing red tip of his Dunhill for a quiet moment. "Quite simply, we cannot let the Fourth Estate anywhere near our treasured guest. They can rant and rave about press privileges all they like, but this is wartime, after all. The government reserves the right to deal with matters of security in any manner it sees fit. That cannot be compromised. It *will* not be. The public, of course, will back us on that all the way down the line."

Simon hesitated. Churchill was absolutely correct. Of course no one could be permitted access to the prisoner. But would it be as simple as that? The clamor for news, for more details surrounding the incident was bound to accelerate, not diminish. As would the questions. Why wasn't the government exploiting the propaganda value of a defecting top-ranking Nazi to full advantage? Surely he had information of great value, mad or not. Why was he being hidden away incommunicado like a leper? What was the government concealing? And what of Hamilton?

"That reporter's not the only loose cannon on the deck, I'm afraid," said Simon.

The prime minister looked at him without speaking.

"We've secured Hamilton's silence for the moment."

"Yes?"

"But both he and Windsor have compromised us badly."

"No one takes Windsor seriously anymore," Churchill said.

"He's been openly sympathetic to the Nazis. There's no question his ultimate goal is to undermine your leadership and reclaim the throne with that wretched wife of his."

"The throne!" Churchill's rising voice chilled the air. "He's disgraced only himself, not England. Damn Windsor and Hamilton too!"

"But . . . forgive me, it's not that simple. There's more. Hamilton's mother-in-law, the Duchess of Northumberland, his brother-in-law Lord Eustice Perry—they're all close to the royal family, Windsor in particular. If we stumble here, they'll waste no time attempting to bring down your government."

"We've nothing to fear from them." Churchill's voice was calmer now. "The English people will not accept a Nazi puppet for a king under any circumstances."

Simon stared at Churchill for a long moment. His mind was made up. It was useless trying to belabor the issue.

"Well," said Simon. "At the moment we can count on Hamilton's cooperation. But I'm afraid that moment may be short-lived if this Hess business gets out of hand."

"Keep him under close watch. Windsor can't do any harm from his post in Bermuda."

"Are we in agreement, then, on what's to be done next?"

Churchill did not hesitate. "I'll send word through Halifax that we accept Hess's proposal. Let him think he has his bloodless victory. I'd make an arrangement with the devil himself if it would help me defeat Adolf Hitler and his pack of barbarians."

CHAPTER TEN

W<small>HEN</small> R<small>UDOLF</small> H<small>ESS</small> arrived at his new home, he was less than pleased. The estate was handsome enough, situated as it was in the midst of lush green mountains thirty miles from Cardiff, not too far from the English border. But what was he doing here? Now that he had delivered his message, he should be permitted to return to the Fatherland.

The van carried him up a snaking dirt road that wound its way through rolling hills surrounded by higher peaks on either side, then stopped in front of a splendid mansion, a truly majestic structure built to last.

Hess looked around, first straight ahead, then to the left and the right. This mansion was now an institution. The sign over the doorway of a nearby red brick building of more recent vintage than the mansion read Monmouthshire Hospital. There were other buildings on the grounds that looked like quarters for hospital personnel. The soldiers motioned for Hess to move forward, into the mansion, which had the name Maindiff Court above its portico.

"What is this place?" Hess said. "Where have you taken me?"

The soldiers looked at one another, then at the man who appeared to be their leader.

"Used to be a loony bin," he said. He looked back at his chums, who were snickering. Hess was furious.

"A psychiatric institute? Is that what you said?"

"Was at one time," the leader said. "It's now a rest home for blokes like us."

"Blokes who've had their fill of fighting Nazis," another soldier said. His glare was meant to be intimidating.

"Come along with you now," the leader said to Hess. "There'll be time enough for yammering later, from what I hear."

Hess marched into the mansion, the guards behind him. His face was ashen, he was stunned. A twitch of panic fluttered his cheek. He was the Deputy Führer of the Third Reich and here he was being marched into an asylum and taunted by riffraff. He would most definitely have to take the matter up with Dr. Guthrie when they met again.

The soldiers escorted their prisoner—for that was how they were treating him—to a comfortable but less than luxurious apartment on the second floor. The leader of the guards told him that someone would be visiting him shortly, then they turned and left him alone.

Hess stepped out onto a terrace that faced the surprisingly high range of mountains. There was a flower garden directly below him. He went back inside and toured the flat, taking in details with his dark, quick-moving eyes. There was an adequate living room, not too large yet not cramped, decorated with modest furniture. Whoever lived here had distinctly bourgeois tastes. The kitchen was fairly large, as was the dining room, and the corner bedroom was particularly light and airy, with two different views of the mountains on the horizon.

Hess did not know it yet, but he was occupying the flat of a Jewish psychiatrist who saw some irony in volunteering his quarters for the internment of England's notorious and unexpected guest.

There was a radio in the living room. Hess, hungering for news of the war, turned it on at once. He did not have to wait long. In the major news story of the day, the commentator informed his listeners that Rudolf Hess had been taken from the Tower of London and moved to an undisclosed location. Further details would be given as soon as they were available.

"Taken from the Tower of London." Did the English public really believe that? The masses, said the Führer, would believe anything if it was repeated often enough. And the Führer had proved it time and time again.

Nothing to do now but wait. Wait for Dr. Guthrie. He had said it would take no longer than forty-eight hours. He was overdue, wasn't he? Hess was losing track of time. This waiting was interminable. He was used to others waiting for him. When he met with Guthrie again he would request—no, demand—that he be returned to his homeland. At once.

PHILIP RENFIELD HAD lost ten pounds in ten weeks, which was not surprising considering the undeniable fact that he ate too little and drank too much. Bachelor life was taking its toll. His clothes hung loosely on his normally lean frame, and the hacking cough that troubled him throughout the brutal Scottish winter refused to fade with the advent of the warm English spring.

For the first time since his separation, he began to feel that perhaps Susan and he could become friends. God, how he hated that word. The truth was, he missed her badly. They could never be just friends. Oddly enough, Susan seemed to be more sympathetic to his frustrations, if not his ambition, now that she didn't have to live with them. She was able to view him tolerantly as a man obsessed rather than as a neglectful husband who preferred the company of strangers in a pub to the comforts of hearth and home. Philip, for his part, missed her in a way he could never have anticipated. Driven as he was, he had depended on her being there when he returned to their small flat after a particularly long day. Susan was a good listener, a sounding board for the ideas he was too close to see objectively. She was also his best editor, something he discovered only after she left. And now her sustaining presence was missing when he needed her more than ever.

After packing her belongings and abandoning him to the dreary rooms they'd shared for most of the last decade, she had traveled down to London and taken a clerical job with a company that manufactured machine-gun parts for the government. Philip was looking forward to their reunion as he pushed his way through the crowds in Piccadilly toward the Boar's Head Public House not far from Susan's office. A partial blackout was still in effect: Most of the shops were open, but the lights inside were dim and curtains were drawn across the window to filter them.

The Boar's Head was familiar ground to Philip, one of his favorite watering holes whenever he was in London. He found the fact that Susan had suggested it somewhat encouraging. He wanted her back. He had been too proud to tell her that before, but he was going to tell her tonight.

The public bar was jammed with early evening drinkers, men his age and older with their ties and collars loosened after a day in the office, and young secretaries in long skirts with fresh makeup on their glowing faces. Most of the young men these days were off in uniform somewhere. Philip threaded his way toward the bar and ordered two double gins with lemon squash, one for himself and one for Susan when she arrived. She never drank anything but gin; he didn't much care what he drank so long as it had alcohol in it.

Susan entered the bar ten minutes later, her thick auburn hair falling in soft waves to her shoulders as she swung her head from side to side looking for him. He caught her eye and pushed his way back through the crowd, the drinks held aloft in either hand. Already, a cluster of single men were closing in on her—which was only to be expected. The shortage of available men during wartime had little impact on women as lovely as his estranged wife.

He stood before her and smiled as she rushed forward to hug him.

"Philip, you've barely any flesh on your bones."

"Here, I ordered for you." He handed her a drink. "Shall we find a table in the private parlor? We've got lots to talk about."

He guided her gently by the arm toward the small room in the rear that was set apart from the noisy barroom. There was something about her that was decidedly different; just what, he wasn't sure. Physically, she hadn't changed a bit. Her skin was as unlined and fair as ever, her figure as trim. There was a vibrancy in her face, an energy current that kept the intensity of her deep blue eyes alive with a kind of ironic intelligence.

The tables were all taken, but there were a couple of spaces on the bench that ran along the wall. Philip took her trench-coat and hung it on the rack, then sat down beside her.

"So. Let me look at you," he said.

"Are you all right, Philip? You look terribly . . . drawn."

"I feel fine, Susan," he said, trying to hold back the racking cough that erupted as soon as he took a drag on his freshly lit cigarette.

"Too many fags," Susan said. She reached for his cigarette, took a drag. It was a habit that had always annoyed him before. Now he found it endearing.

"Too many fags, too much booze, too much everything except you. I need more Susan in my life."

"Don't, Philip." She looked away. "Don't make this more difficult than it is."

"I mean that, you know. I miss you terribly. I want you back. There, I've said it."

"We've been through this before, Philip. I can't go back to that life again."

"It'll be different this time. I swear it. I've changed."

"For how long? A month? Three months? You can't change, darling. You're the way you are and that's all you can be. All *any* of us can be. You'd be miserable if you tried to change for me."

"I'm miserable now, so what's the difference?"

"I'm going to leave, Philip. I can't take any more of this."

"Don't go. Please. I'll let it go for now. I've got to talk to you about something else, something quite incredible. I think I'm onto the biggest story I've ever gone after, and I may be in a bit of trouble as a result."

"What story? What kind of trouble?"

The waitress came by to gather up the empty glasses and Philip ordered two more double gins.

"This Hess business," Philip said. "I suppose you've been following it?"

"Who hasn't? I meant to congratulate you—I know you broke the story."

"No matter, I wish I hadn't. Sometimes I wish I'd bloody

well never heard of Rudolf Hess or the Duke of Hamilton or anyone else involved in this sinister mess."

"What are you driving at?"

"For starters, that bloke they were displaying in the Tower of London until yesterday wasn't Rudolf Hess. I don't know who he was, but I damned well know who he wasn't."

"I don't understand, Philip. Why would the government say he was Hess if he wasn't? What's to be gained by it?"

The waitress returned with their drinks. Philip paid for them, then lit another cigarette from his crumpled pack.

"The why of it I haven't figured out yet," he said. He exhaled smoke and passed the cigarette to Susan, who inhaled deeply without taking her eyes from his. "But I do know this. There was a swap done up at Maryhill Barracks. The chap they escorted into a lorry and transported to London wasn't Hess. The real Hess was taken out under guard a half hour later and brought to a posh residence in Pollockshields. I saw it all with my own eyes."

Susan stared into Philip's face for a long moment, took his cigarette and slipped it between her lips. Philip, warmed by this, the only remaining intimacy they shared, suddenly understood what was different about her. This Susan who now lived without him no longer needed him. Their roles were reversed. It was he who grasped at symbolic gestures, he who was trying to preserve the fragile threads of a relationship.

"You say you observed this deception yourself?"

"I lingered across from Maryhill after the other reporters left to file their stories and I recognized the real Hess from photographs I'd seen before. They took Hess to Pollockshields, but I don't imagine they'll keep him there very long. They'll want him someplace safe and sound." Philip gave in to another of his deep-throated coughs; Susan reached across to comfort him, then drew her hand back.

"You can touch me if you like," he said. "It's quite all right."

"You said you think you're in some sort of trouble," she said. "Why?"

"For one thing, I'm being followed."

"You're sure?"

"I'm not paranoid, Susan. At least, not without reason. Paranoia, as you know, is my first line of defense. But in this case they're not even trying to conceal it."

Susan's eyes darted around the smoke-filled room.

"Not to worry," he said. "I gave them the slip in Glasgow, they're off my scent—for the moment, at least."

"But *who*, Philip?"

"My guess is British intelligence. Apparently her majesty's government is not exactly pleased with my blowing the whistle on the Hess story and has decided to monitor my activities. They've closed off the newspaper to me, you know. The order came right down from your father. He's got me reporting what the Ladies' League of Glasgow is doing to help in the war effort."

"What on earth do you think is going on?"

"I told you, I haven't figured that out yet. But I don't believe for one minute that Hess's flight was the bizarre act of a madman. He botched it, that's all. But the whole thing was prearranged, possibly by Hamilton—for what reason, one can only guess."

"Philip, listen to me. Please. *Stop* guessing. You're the most dedicated journalist I've ever known—no one knows that better than I—but this dedication of yours has pushed you over the edge. Whatever is going on in the top levels of government is all for the good—it *must* be. You've got to drop this, Philip."

"Wait a minute. How can a secret, prearranged visit from the Deputy Führer of a country that's been bombing hell out of us be for the good? What good can come from the government's parading a decoy while hiding the real thing somewhere else? Whatever's going on here we have a right to know. And as a reporter I have an obligation to—"

"Get yourself killed?" She mashed out his half-smoked cigarette without offering it back to him. "You're a stubborn fool, always have been. Sticking your nose where it doesn't belong, when it's obvious there has to be a valid reason for all of this. How can you think for one minute that Churchill has some sinister design?"

"I don't know *what* his design is. But I'm damned well going to find out."

"Well you'll have to find out on your own. I want no part of it."

"That's not how your father feels." As soon as he said it, he wished he hadn't.

"What do you mean? I thought he'd closed off the paper to you?"

"He had no choice in that; government orders, you know. But he knows I'm onto something big and he wants it. He's financing me out of his own pocket—for later." Was he telling her this just to hurt her?

She stared at him. Her eyes were moist and there was redness in her cheeks.

"I'm sorry," he said. "I shouldn't have told you that."

She looked away.

"Well," she said. "You always did get on with him better than I."

"Damn it, Susan! I had to talk to *you*. I know I haven't been a good husband, but I miss you so much. You've always been there for me, you always know what to do. I never realized before how much I depended on that."

Susan's blue eyes looked unnaturally bright. He watched the battle for self-control, a battle she almost won.

"It hasn't been easy for me, either," she said. "Seeing you again tonight is quite difficult for me."

"Do you . . . do you still . . ."

"I can't allow myself to love you any longer," she said softly. "I can't permit that, ever again. But I *do* care what happens to you, and I'm begging you to drop this thing—now, before it's too late."

"I can't drop it, Susan. I just can't do that. It's all I have left now."

"Well then, my darling, I can't help. I know my father better than you do. He'll use you as long as it suits him, then cut you free. When that happens, you won't have him left either. Take care of yourself, will you? I have to go now."

Philip nodded. He watched Susan retrieve her coat and walk out the side door into the darkening evening. He finished off the remains of his gin and pulled the packet of cigarettes out of the hip pocket of his worn jacket. He started to light one, then thought better of it and put it back. He headed toward the barroom to order another drink, then decided against that as well and left through the door Susan had used just moments before.

Philip Renfield had never felt so utterly desolate in his entire life, not even when Susan walked out on him. Then, he'd assumed he would get along well enough without her. Now he knew better. His black mood so consumed him that he failed to notice the solitary figure slip out of the doorway across the street and fall in behind him as he threaded his way back toward the heart of Piccadilly.

CHAPTER ELEVEN

ALL THIS TIME and nothing to do but wait. Rudolf Hess paced the room, twelve steps ahead, twelve steps back, eight across, eight back. He was used to being busy. Busy with his drawing, with his garden, with his literary pursuits. So many talents and no way to display them since he arrived in Scotland. History demanded something of him. He must continue to work on his diary. A record. A document. A journal for posterity. He must set all his thoughts down on paper. All the things he knew. They must be preserved. If he failed to set the record straight, who would do it? He was the one. Fate had selected him to chronicle the Third Reich—just as it had selected him to edit the Führer's masterwork. He began to write:

Following a successful military career, Karl Haushofer became a professor of geopolitics at Munich University. Among his students was the author—I, Rudolf Hess—who eventually introduced the geographer and former general to my friend,

Adolf Hitler. Haushofer's ideas on geopolitics had a great influence on Hitler, and this influence was much in evidence in Hitler's seminal work, *Mein Kampf*. As Hitler's National Socialist movement grew in Germany through the 1920s and into the 1930s, Haushofer's power as a theorist and top adviser to our leader expanded with it.

Both Haushofer and I regarded Hitler as the destined savior of Germany. Each in our own way contributed to Adolf Hitler's vision of himself as "the greatest German who ever lived," Haushofer with his intellectual influence, and I with my total dedication to Hitler. It was I who defended Hitler with my fists against the Bolsheviks during the beer-house rallies in Munich in the 1920s. Hitler valued such fierce loyalty more than any other trait among his followers.

With Haushofer's intellectual guidance, and my editorial assistance, Hitler informed the world in *Mein Kampf* that Germany's dreams of territorial expansion to the east could be accomplished only if it avoided fighting a simultaneous battle on its western flank. Of Hitler's top advisers, I was the only one with serious cultural achievements. I had read widely and written many articles and pamphlets, and I knew music and art. It was therefore only natural that Hitler would turn to me to assist him with his manuscript, which he originally wanted to call *Four and a Half Years of Struggle against Lies, Stupidity, and Cowardice*. It was I who convinced him to shorten it to *Mein Kampf*.

When the book appeared after round-the-clock rewriting on my battered old Remington typewriter, it was recognized by all thinking people as an important historical masterwork. In *Mein Kampf*, Hitler set forth his blueprint for the annihilation of bourgeois democracy and the supremacy of the German race. Hitler concealed nothing in *Mein Kampf*. In effect, he said to the world, "This is who I am and this is what I intend to do." Like Machiavelli's *The Prince*, *Mein Kampf* denounced the author's enemies and called for a new world order based on pure German values, a renewed sense of pride, a free and independent German spirit and morality. To achieve this, Germany would have to purge itself of all things foreign and alien that had been destroying our people like a disease from within.

As early as the mid-1920s, Hitler believed that England was too effete to stand up to a rearmed and reinvigorated Germany. He resisted the advice of his military advisers, and refused to deal England a final crushing blow that would have taken her out of the war completely because he thought it would not be necessary. The Führer firmly believed that the bloodless defeat of England, and the installation of the Duke of Windsor, who was sympathetic to Germany's goals, as its monarch was within his grasp.

Only Churchill stood in his way. Churchill, the obstinate bulldog, was the only remaining hurdle standing between Germany and its historical destiny. If only the Führer could bend Churchill to his will, he would be free to turn eastward and achieve his goal of territorial expansion. Karl Haushofer informed the Führer that the key to Churchill was the Duke of Hamilton, not the Duke of Windsor, whose open sympathies for Germany were somewhat suspect with most of the British public.

I concurred. Even those in the royal family who supported Windsor's views were too afraid to come forward publicly. We knew that Churchill despised the former king, and would do anything he could to silence him. But the Duke of Hamilton did have Churchill's respect. He kept his views on Germany largely to himself, and was a more suitable spokesman for Hitler's peace proposal.

Hamilton and I had developed an understanding of sorts during our meeting at the Olympic Games in Berlin in 1936. Unlike the Duke of Windsor, he was guarded in his public comments, a trait that made him potentially more valuable as an emissary to the British government. Karl Haushofer and his son Albrecht commenced a correspondence with Hamilton that continued for several years. Hamilton had met both of them in Munich. The letters from the Haushofers were usually forwarded through a Mrs. Roberts in Lisbon to lessen the chances of British intelligence intercepting them. Karl Haushofer's wife is a Jew, and she, Albrecht, and another son named Heinz carry letters of immunity signed by Hitler himself because of their great value to the Reich and their loyalty to the Führer.

England's great hope in this war has been the eventual support of the United States, but this is an unlikely dream. Even there Germany has her friends. The American airman Charles Lindbergh has been making speeches all over the United States, advising his fellow Americans to stay out of the war. Henry Ford ships steel to us from his factory in England, and Ambassador Joseph Kennedy constantly advises Roosevelt to let Europe and England go it alone without American help. All of them were personally decorated by the Führer at his home near Berchtesgaden, and Kennedy is a frequent customer at my brothel on Giesenrechs Strasse in Berlin. If he should ever become a problem, he is certainly vulnerable in that area.

So, it seems, the whole world is willing to turn the other cheek while Germany extends her borders eastward—and rids the world of Bolshevism while we're doing it. Everyone but Churchill. In 1937 the Duke of Hamilton arranged for Albrecht Haushofer to deliver a lecture at Chatham House in London, explaining our point of view. In the course of his speech, he blamed England for many of Germany's problems following the Treaty of Versailles. Afterward, he visited Hamilton at Dungavel Castle in Glasgow, the estate where I attempted to land my Messerschmitt 110.

WHEN WINSTON CHURCHILL received the latest Reuters dispatch from his secretary, he studied the report with a fascination bordering on horror. There had never been any doubt in Churchill's mind that Hitler was evil incarnate—one of the most ruthless and amoral men who ever lived. He had yet to honor any agreement he had ever made, and Churchill had no illusions about Hitler honoring one with him. But the lengths he would go to in order to further his own ends were truly amazing.

According to German news reports, Hess's adjutant Karl Pintch had been arrested and imprisoned in Munich for conspiracy in the planning of Hess's "unauthorized flight" to Scotland; Rudolf Hess's wife Ilse, herself a longtime friend of the Führer, was being held under house arrest and investigated for complicity in her husband's flight. Most horrifying of all, the entire Haushofer family had been seized by the Gestapo for concealing their Jewish heritage and poisoning the mind of the Deputy Führer of the Third Reich.

There was no question that Rudolf Hess himself, perhaps Hitler's closest friend and most loyal follower, would meet a similar end if he were shipped back to Germany. He had made the fatal mistake of bungling his mission, and that one mistake carried more weight than all the years of slavish loyalty Hess had given to the greatest German who ever lived.

CHAPTER TWELVE

Hᴉᴛʟᴇʀ ᴡᴀs ᴅʀɪɴᴋɪɴɢ tea—tepid, dark and diluted heavily with cream. A tray of cream cakes and other sweets sat on his desk. As usual, he had herded his deputies into the tiny study on the first floor. Göring, Goebbels and Himmler sat cramped together across from Hitler, who stood beside his desk. Goebbels was all but crushed between the two massive men.

Hitler began pacing back and forth in the small space in front of the men, eyes blazing, lank dark hair hanging down the left side of his brow. In one hand he held a dispatch from the embassy in Ireland, Churchill's reply to his proposal. He waved it in front of him like a demented conductor leading an orchestra.

"This!" he screamed. He slapped the paper with the back of his free hand. "This is his answer to our message!"

In effect, the dispatch said that England would agree not to engage Germany on the continent while Operation Barbarossa was in progress—but that a cessation of all hostilities between the two nations was out of the question. England would continue to pursue its campaign in North Africa and, possibly, extend it into Italy until a more viable peace agreement could be reached. If this was acceptable to the Third Reich, Germany could proceed to transfer the 200 divisions in the west plus the panzer and Luftwaffe forces to its eastern borders without fear of reprisal from England. In the meantime, Rudolf Hess would be well provided for in England, since his return to Germany would compromise England's integrity.

"This . . . this pigshit is his answer!" Hitler stormed back to his desk.

"But, my Führer," said Göring, "if you please, they are conceding our main point. They are giving us the breathing space we need to conquer the east. For the sake of appearances they must not give the impression that they have capitulated completely. Churchill's government would collapse under the weight of world opinion—"

"And we'd have what we want!" Hitler said. "A bloodless surrender. A neutral state, a friendly state with our own people in power."

"Yes, but—" Göring looked from Goebbels to Himmler, hoping for support, but it was not forthcoming. "Eventually, but not now," he said. "Eventually England will retire from the war, when she sees it is futile to continue a losing battle. But for now, we are free to begin the invasion of Russia."

Hitler spat the words out. "Do you trust Churchill?"

"Of course not, my Führer. But—"

"As soon as we accept his offer, he will notify Stalin and ship arms to Moscow."

"Yes, but we will surprise him, Führer," Himmler put in. "By the time his arms arrive, we shall be there to receive them."

Hitler twisted his mouth into what passed for a smile.

"What are our options?" Goebbels said. "We can refuse Churchill's offer, or we can work our plan in stages. Russia first, then the conquest of England—before the Americans come to Churchill's aid."

Hitler, unblinking, stared at each of them in turn through a long silence.

"I have decided," he said finally. "We will proceed with the invasion. The generals are coming tonight for a nine o'clock meeting in the map room."

Göring turned to Himmler, to Goebbels, then back to Hitler, who answered his unvoiced question.

"I decided this before you arrived, Herr Göring."

TIRED OF LISTENING to his radio, Rudolf Hess pulled out his journal and wrote:

I joined the party in 1919, a few weeks after Alfred Rosenberg, a Balt from Reval who had been trained as an architect but considered himself to be a philosopher after publishing a book called *The Myth of the Twentieth Century*, a work of such monumental dullness that even the Führer could not read it in its entirety. Despite his intellectual pretensions, Rosenberg was committed to Hitler and his emerging political philosophy, and the three of us formed the nucleus of the movement that was later to attract Göring, Goebbels, Heinrich Himmler and Julius Streicher to its ranks. Rosenberg always swore to the Führer that he was not Jewish, and that the name Rosenberg was common among Christians in the Estonian section of Russia. If anything, he detested Jews even more than the Führer did, and he contributed a scientific basis for his genetic views for distribution by the Party.

By the early 1920s, when he was still in his early thirties, Adolf Hitler had perfected his oratorical talents to such a degree that he was able to do with his audience exactly as he pleased. After an early career as an artist of some note in Austria, he found his true calling as the greatest political leader in history—a man blessed with the vision and the ability to lead an entire nation to the fulfillment of its historical destiny. He gave eloquent voice to the frustrations of the entire German people with threads of pure logic and reason. No one of intelligence could dispute his premises and deductions.

Among the Führer's disciples, no one was more committed to him—or closer to him— than I. Many of those who later joined the Party were simple unskilled workers who needed a leader to turn to, someone who expressed in public what they felt in their hearts. The first major test of Hitler's growing strength came during a rally at the Hofbrauhaus in Munich on November 4, 1921. The hall was packed with 700 Communists spoiling for a fight, and we arrived—only forty-two in number—dressed in ski caps, gray Bavarian coats with red armbands, knee breeches and thick woolen socks. We were the forerunners to the SA and SS troops who came later.

After speaking for the better part of an hour, Hitler was interrupted by a rowdy Communist worker from one of the local factories. He answered back, and beer mugs started flying through the air in Hitler's direction. The Führer gave the order to respond in kind and teach the Bolsheviks a lesson. "Respond without cowardice!" he commanded. As one, we charged the rabble-rousers without concern about their greater numbers. I was proud to lead the assault, and I can tell you the fighting continued without letup for twenty minutes. Finally, our small army, armed with chair legs, beer mugs and fists, routed the disorganized Communists from the hall. The bloodied heads, smashed furniture and broken glass testified to the courage and dedication of our small band. We knew then that nothing could stop us from that moment on. Our commitment to our cause and to our leader would surmount all opposition.

Rudolf Hess laid down his pen, rubbed his eyes and pushed his chair back from the desk. How easily it all came back to him. It had always been this way. He had only to take a pen in hand, and the creative juices began to flow. The floodgates opened, the memories poured out.

Thank God he had this journal to work on. It was important to set the record straight. Every great movement needed its historian. Adolf Hitler had been chosen by the gods to lead Germany to its historical destiny. And he, Rudolf Hess, had been likewise chosen to help the Führer accomplish his mission, and to set down these philosophical truths so that the world could understand them in their historical perspective.

But it was time now that he returned to the Fatherland. Why had Dr. Guthrie kept him waiting? Why was he isolated like this? Rudolf Hess was not a patient man. If Guthrie did not call on him within the next twenty-four hours, he would demand an explanation from the prime minister himself.

CHAPTER THIRTEEN

AT THE BERGHOF, no one spoke while Hitler ate. The generals picked at their food and stole furtive glances at one another from time to time while Hitler wolfed down one of the heavy meals he loved so much: corn on the cob drenched with butter that oozed along his fingers, Viennese pancakes sprinkled with sugar and raisins and drowned with a gelatinous sweet sauce, and sausages. Meat, when he took it, was always in the form of sausages that accompanied his pancakes. He drank light beer tonight, a warning to everyone in attendance to be on guard. Nothing darkened Hitler's moods more quickly than alcohol.

Seated around the banquet table were Göring; General Gerd von Rundstedt, who irritated the Führer with his bleating Anglophilia; General Gunther Blumentritt, who, Hitler suspected, had criticized his conduct of the war behind his back; General Heinrich Walter von Brauchitsch, who also believed that Hitler's unrelenting hostility toward the western powers was doomed to failure; General Franz Halder, who secretly detested the swaggering Göring as well as the violent excesses of the SS; Field Marshall Fritz Erich von Manstein, who had already tried unsuccessfully to convince the Führer that a war against Russia would be a bitter one, even with British cooperation; and General Friedrich von Paulus, perhaps the most blindly loyal to Hitler within the group.

Hitler ate in silence, enjoying the nervous quietude that permeated the dining room with an almost palpable presence. He had long despised the professional military class, had hated the generals and their superior ways ever since he was a starving corporal in World War I. He particularly enjoyed his power over them now.

He pushed his empty dishes away, drained his glass of the remaining drops of beer, and stared directly into von Rundstedt's eyes. Hitler believed that by looking into a man's eyes you could see his soul, know everything there was to know about him.

"So you think the English are such civilized people," Hitler said. "You think they are a race equal to our own, a race worthy of sharing world power with the Reich."

"No, no, my Führer," von Rundstedt said. Embarrassed, he looked around at the others for support, then turned back to Hitler. "It is only that I think there is . . . stability, yes that's the word, stability in the British Empire. Not equality, Führer, but order and stability that can serve our own ends."

"Rubbish!" Hitler said. "Let me tell you about your beloved British. They are not like Germans at all. They are indolent and morally degenerate. Let me tell you about the plans I have for England after Russia has fallen. These rules and regulations that I am having prepared, 'Orders Concerning the Organization and Function of the Military Government of England,' are irrevocable. The German army of occupation will remain permanently on English soil. Able-bodied English males between seventeen and forty-five are to be put to work for the Third Reich—in Germany and the eastern lands.

"English culture will be totally assimilated into the Reich. We will encourage intermarriage so that within a generation or two we will have produced a new race of Anglo-Germans that will be incorporated into the ruling class. The SS presence will be felt—with offices in all major cities: London, Bristol, Birmingham, Liverpool, Manchester and Edinburgh. We have no use for the Jews, of course, and the intellectuals. Our plans for the occupation are being readied. I've instructed Herr Professor Franz Six to set it all up. That, my dear General von Rundstedt, is what I think of your English."

Hitler stood up. He looked directly into the eyes of Blumentritt, then the others one by one except for Paulus, whom he considered a nonentity, and Göring, whom he trusted.

"Essentially, everything depends on me," Hitler said. "Everything depends on my existence, my activity."

Hitler's men had seen and heard it all before, watched him act out his demonic fantasies with subtle variations time after time, knew it was senseless to try to interrupt him. Senseless and potentially suicidal.

"No one will ever have the confidence of the entire German people as I have it, never again. Never again will one man come along who commands more power and authority than I."

The generals were silent, their faces impassive.

"My existence is therefore indispensable in the success of our mission."

Hitler turned and faced his men directly. "But even I can be eliminated at any time by a criminal or an idiot."

He held their gaze for a long moment. No one moved, no one spoke.

Finally, after this startling diatribe—discourse that was so effective before his mass audiences and so numbing and disturbing at close range—Hitler arrived at his main point.

"We've set the date. At seven o'clock on the morning of June twenty-second, I will address the German people and inform them that Operation Barbarossa is under way. I will tell them that I have decided to place the fate and future of the Reich and our people in the hands of our soldiers. We have only to kick in the door to Russia, and the whole rotten structure will come crashing down."

The generals were stunned to a man—even Göring, privy to most of the Führer's private plans. Everyone knew that war with Russia was on the horizon, but could the entire Wehrmacht be mobilized in a month?

"Führer, may I comment?" Göring said finally.

"Go on." Hitler's eyes were blazing, his smile almost beatific.

"June twenty-second, my Führer? Would it perhaps be better to wait until our Suez offensive is complete?"

"I've had enough of Mediterranean adventures. The destruction of Egypt can wait until Russia is defeated, which, I expect, will be October at the latest. The Luftwaffe is ready, is it not?"

"Of course."

"And our armies are fresh and ready to march?"

"Indeed they are," Paulus said. He looked around the table, daring the others to contradict him.

"Why wait any longer then?" Hitler said. "Already we're two weeks behind schedule. June twenty-second is the next favorable date. I will not be put off any longer."

Even Göring, committed to the Führer as he was, did not believe that the fate of the Third Reich should be dictated by planetary aspects. If Churchill knew of the Führer's obsession, he presumably had stargazers of his own telling him of

Germany's likely timetable. But it was impossible to dissuade Hitler once his mind was made up.

"The Luftwaffe awaits your command," Göring said.

"The infantry and armored divisions will be ready," Paulus said.

"Are we unanimous then?" Hitler asked. He directed his question primarily to the others, who fidgeted uncomfortably. Hitler, they all knew, would accept nothing less than their explicit and unqualified agreement.

Von Rundstedt frowned, then swallowed deeply. "My troops will be ready as you wish, my Führer," he said.

One by one, the others voiced their compliance. Hitler's face shone, his eyes moist with tears.

"We're not simply going to conquer Russia," Hitler said, "we're going to wipe her from the map. In a few short weeks we'll be in Moscow. There is absolutely no doubt about it. I will raze that damnable city to the ground, and turn it into an artificial sea big enough to supply all our energy needs in the east. Moscow will vanish forever. Then Stalingrad, Kiev and St. Petersburg. All of them."

The generals had been trained in the art of combat. All of them regarded warfare as a noble profession, perhaps the noblest of all. But where was the nobility in total annihilation? Never before had they been asked to satisfy the emotional needs of a single, obsessive, insatiable individual. Not until this moment.

CHAPTER FOURTEEN

June 1941

"THE LAST THING we need now is an early victory for either side," Churchill said. He was unusually jumpy today, rising from his cushioned chair and pacing behind it, sitting down, then rising and pacing all over again.

"I agree," Simon said. "A victorious Stalin in Germany is no more desirable than a victorious Hitler in Moscow, free to turn his attention on us."

"It must be prolonged, it's the only way. That will give us time to rebuild our defenses, finish the business in North Africa, and get the Americans into it. It's just a question of time now."

Sir John Simon studied the prime minister, trying to read his next thought from every facial tic. Simon ordinarily looked ten to fifteen years younger than his sixty-eight years, but today he was feeling his age.

"We're all set with Cripps, I assume," Churchill said.

"He's already spoken to Stalin along the lines we discussed. So far, the plan's unfolding without a wrinkle."

"Damn that Cripps! We can't trust him either. He's a Bolshie himself in a tweed suit. Too cozy with Stalin for my tastes."

"True. But he doesn't know anything, and he accepted our story at face value. As far as he—and Stalin—are concerned, Hitler will attack *after* he's finished with us. We'll ship him arms to help him hold up his end against the Wehrmacht. Ideally, the net result will be a stalemate."

"It's risky, John. Damned risky," Churchill said.

"Risky but necessary. We have no other options. Besides, there's no reason it should fail."

Churchill laughed. "I can think of a dozen reasons," he said. "But you're right, it's the only course left to us. This Hess affair is nerve-racking too. When are you meeting with him again?"

"Tomorrow, I should think. I'm leaving for Wales tonight. There's no hurry, actually. It's all been set up through Halifax. Talking to Hess about it is a formality."

"It's important to keep him under wraps. We don't need any unpleasant surprises on his end."

"I'll speak to him tomorrow, make sure he's well treated, content. Ease his mind, so to speak."

"No need to coddle him too much," Churchill said. "He's powerless as long as he's isolated. Be sure to question him thoroughly, using any means you think best. Make it clear he's not returning anywhere unless he supplies us with any information we ask for. Bully him if you have to."

"You can be sure of it," Simon said, "although, judging by his pathetically bloated ego, I rather think a sugar-coated approach might be more effective at first. Particularly if he thinks we're allies now."

The prime minister smiled, seeming almost to relax.

"Well, my dear Doctor Guthrie," he said. "We've done all we can do. It's in the hands of the Almighty now. All we can do is trust in him."

"In him and in the gullibility of our friends and enemies alike," Simon said.

"I'VE SOMETHING FOR you, Philip," Buchanan said. "It concerns our private business." Buchanan looked left and right, then back at his son-in-law. "You'd better step into my office."

Philip Renfield followed the older man into his inner sanctum. Buchanan waited at the door for Philip to step inside, then shut the door behind him.

"Sit down, this might take a minute."

Buchanan was tall and lean and sinewy at sixty-six years of age. He was handsome in a weather-beaten way, cheeks red and lined, his hair still mostly deep red on top and turning whitish at the temples. Susan's resemblance to her father was unmistakable. Amazing how two people who looked so much alike could get on so poorly. Buchanan sat down behind his desk and swung his legs up onto an open drawer.

"Tired of covering the ladies' tea circuit?" Buchanan said. There was an impish smile on his lips.

"My idea of hell," Philip said, "is spending eternity doing just that."

Buchanan smiled openly, then abruptly furrowed his brow.

"Yes, well," he said, "I have something more urgent for you to look into. Concerns this Hess affair."

Philip leaned forward in his seat.

"Could be significant," Buchanan said, "or it could be nothing at all. That's for you to find out."

"What is it?"

"A friend of mine just returned from Wales on holiday. Stayed with his wife at the Angel Hotel, a few miles down the road from Monmouthshire Hospital about fifty kilometers outside of Cardiff. Monmouthshire used to be a psychiatric hospital before the war. Now it's been converted to an isolation camp of sorts, primarily for military personnel who've cracked up in combat."

"I had no idea," Philip said.

"The government's not too keen on word getting out," Buchanan said. "Bad for morale and that sort of thing. Anyway, this chap was in the hotel pub one night and engaged an officer posted at the hospital in conversation. Couldn't get away from him, he said. The officer was two gins past his limit and ranted on and on about a new guest at the facility, a Gerry supposedly, all very hush-hush according to him."

"Hess?" Philip said.

"Wouldn't say, or couldn't," Buchanan said. "Apparently, the only modicum of discretion the officer displayed all evening. Soon as I heard about it, I thought you'd best go down and find out what it's all about. How soon can you leave?"

"I'm on my way," Philip said. "I'll take the afternoon train. Won't take me five minutes to pack."

"Be careful, Philip," Buchanan said. "I'm concerned about your personal safety, of course. And we don't want to alert the government that we're prying into something they'd rather we didn't."

"No need to worry about me. Precaution is my middle name."

As Philip was about to leave, Buchanan called out to him, "How are you and Susan getting on lately, if you don't mind my asking?"

"Not well, I'm afraid. She's tired of playing second fiddle to a story. She won't reconsider."

"Sorry to hear that," Buchanan said. "She's as obstinate as her mother. I'm sure I don't have to tell you, Philip, not a word of this to anyone, including my daughter."

*   *   *

HE ARRIVED TIRED and hungry at seven o'clock in the evening, and checked into a room at the hotel. All that was available in the dining room was a light dinner of bacon, eggs and fried tomatoes that he ate quickly and washed down with a pot of scalding tea. Then he retired to the public room and chatted up the barman while he waited.

The officer he was looking for didn't come into the pub alone until the following night. He was a short barrel of a man with a round florid face and straight black hair, younger than Philip by several years. Three elderly men huddled together at the far end of the bar, local pensioners by the look of them, smoking and nursing their pints of beer. Philip waited until the officer finished his first gin, then turned to him.

"Been posted out here long, have you?" Philip said.

"Too bloody long if you ask me," the officer said. He motioned to the barman. "Let's have another, Tom."

"Have one on me. I'll have another pint as well." Philip raised his empty glass to Tom. "I'm only too happy to buy a round or two for the boys in uniform."

"Don't mind if I do," the officer said. He extended his hand. "Leftenant Harry Wilkins."

"Charles Rogers. Pleased to know you."

"What brings you to these parts? I detect a touch of Scots in your voice, if I'm not mistaken."

"I'm on holiday, if you can call it that. The missus and I've just split, actually. Needed to get off by myself for a while and sort things out."

"Sorry to hear it. Love 'em and leave 'em, that's my philosophy. Soon as you settle in with them, they think they bloody well own you."

"They do at that, don't they," Philip said. "I won't be too quick to do it again, I tell you. I don't suppose you've much of a problem with females out here."

"Hah! The only ones I've seen in a year are over sixty and homely as Aunt Harriet."

"Fag?" Philip extended his pack, then erupted in a coughing fit as soon as he lit one for himself.

"One vice is as bad as another," Wilkins said. He inhaled deeply on the cigarette and drained the remains of his gin. Philip called for another round.

"I take it you're posted up at Monmouthshire," Philip said. "Used to be a home for loonies, didn't it?"

"So they tell me. Nothing but soldiers up there now, soldiers on rehab who've lost their stomach for the war. Enough to drive anyone starkers."

"Oh?"

"I was beginning to lose my own mind until I lucked into this cushy assignment about a week ago."

"That so?"

Leftenant Wilkins looked around at the locals, then leaned closer to Philip.

"This is strictly between you, me and the bar stool," he said, "but there's something not quite right going on up there."

"What do you mean?"

"A week back a new visitor arrived—very mysterious, mind you, no name, a tall chap wearing a muffler around his neck and a floppy hat low on his face. Moved him into a flat that was vacated by one of the quacks on staff. He's been isolated since, no contact with anyone except the old dear who makes his bed and cooks his meals. And me."

"Hows that?"

"A day after he settled in, I was assigned to be his driver. Howling mad at first, I was—an officer with combat time ordered to be somebody's batman—until I realized this was no ordinary duty."

Philip finished his beer, ordered another round and lit cigarettes for both of them. He had his man rolling now. There was no way to stop him from spinning his yarn even if he'd wanted to.

"I wasn't told in so many words," the leftenant said, "but it didn't take me long to put two and two together. This was no ordinary bloke. Smooth. Educated. An air of authority about him. Spoke English with a slight German accent. And no wonder: The chap I'm driving about is none other than that flippin' Nazi who crashed his plane up in your end of the forest."

"Surely you're joking," Philip said.

"There's no question about it. His picture's been all over the papers. That one they stuck up in the Tower of London's a bloody impostor."

"But why on earth . . ."

"There's something going on that's not right, I'm telling you. Something they're trying to keep from the public."

"This is positively incredible."

"He seems like a right decent sort too, I don't mind telling you. We're fighting the wrong country if you ask me. We should be helping the Gerries mop up the Bolshies instead of the other way around. Churchill's got it ass over teakettle and we'll pay for it later, you can mark my words on that."

A few more locals entered the pub, ordered pints and carried them to a table near the stove. The three pensioners were still crowded around their drinks down at the end. Laughter from the new arrivals filled the pub and waves of blue-gray cigarette smoke curled in the air. Philip ordered another round for Wilkins, nothing for himself this time.

"Perhaps you're right," he said.

"I know I'm right. We're getting bombed all to hell for nothing. To hell with the bloody frogs, let them fend for themselves. Let the Gerries clean up the Bolshies and do what they want with the continent."

"You don't think they'd turn on us later?"

"Not if they've nothing to fear. I've been chatting it up with this Gerry quite a bit, I have. Drove him down to Whitecastle so he could soak up the sun, then over to Llanthony Abbey to peek at the ruins."

Leftenant Wilkins, Philip knew, was referring to the eleventh-century medieval castle complete with moat and drawbridge and the twelfth-century church destroyed by Oliver Cromwell centuries after it was built.

"Nothing to do but talk," the leftenant said. "He grew up with Brits in North Africa, says we're all the same race—all Aryans, he says. We should be pulling together to keep the kikes and darkies in line instead of killing each other. I don't mind telling you, I don't have much to say against that."

Philip took a deep drag on his cigarette and went into a spasm of coughing. One day soon he would give up the nasty habit, but he had too much to think about now, too much more to do. When this whole business was behind him, the horror and destruction, he'd change his ways, eat proper meals, cut back on beer and cigarettes. Take some exercise too.

The leftenant drained his glass, stood up from the stool. "Much obliged . . . Charles, is it?" he said. "Got to be getting back to camp. Taking his nibs for a stroll around the grounds tomorrow. Bright-eyed and bushy-tailed and all that sort of thing."

"It's been a pleasure," Philip said. "Do you get down here often? Perhaps we can continue our conversation while I'm still on holiday."

"Don't see why not. I expect I can pop down for an hour tomorrow evening. Eightish or thereabouts?"

"I look forward to it," Philip said. "See you then."

Leftenant Wilkins hiccuped, placed his hat at an odd angle on the back of his head, and threaded his way uncertainly toward the exit. Philip watched him sway through the door, then turned back and occupied himself with the remains of his beer. Two of the pensioners at the end of the bar said cheerio to their mate and walked out into the night. Philip thought nothing of it, finished his drink, left a ten-bob note for the barman, then retired to his room to make notes of his conversation with the officer.

PHILIP RENFIELD SPENT the following evening drinking by himself until closing time at ten-thirty. Leftenant Wilkins did not return.

Philip felt a sense of disquiet as he climbed the stairs to his room. The only other drinker in the pub had been the solitary pensioner who had been left alone by his friends the previous night. The pensioner was the last to leave—and hadn't he been the last to leave the night before? Philip did not know why that should bother him, but it kept him from sleeping except in fits and starts until his bedside alarm went off at seven o'clock.

He dressed and went downstairs to a breakfast of porridge drenched with canned milk and toasted biscuits. When he finished eating, he walked through the hotel lobby to the public telephone across from the reception desk. He looked up the number of Monmouthshire Hospital, closed the kiosk door behind him, and dialed it.

"I'd like to speak to Leftenant Wilkins," he said to the operator who answered.

"Who's calling?"

"Charles Rogers. I'm a friend of his."

"Just one moment, please."

Philip fiddled with his pen while he waited for the operator to come back on the line.

"I'm sorry, Mr. Rogers, but Leftenant Wilkins is no longer posted at this base," she said.

He was speechless for a long moment.

"Hello? Sir?"

"Yes, yes, I'm here. But that's impossible. I . . . I was just talking to him day before last. He told me nothing about any transfer."

"He's no longer here, sir."

"Where's he gone to then?"

"I'm not at liberty to say."

"That's bizarre," Philip said. "Transferred on a moment's notice like that, no advance warning or anything."

"I'm afraid that's all the information I have."

"Where does he live? I have to get a message to him, it's urgent."

"It will be forwarded along to him if you send it here, sir. I can't divulge personal—"

"Good God!" Philip rang off before she could finish. What was going on, anyway? Some kind of top-secret charade? Whatever it was, he vowed to uncover it if it killed him.

The government was hiding the real Rudolf Hess from the world. Why? Why didn't it want anyone to speak to him? What could he say that would be so damaging? Was he really a madman who'd flown off on his own? Apparently not. If he were, Churchill's government wouldn't be hiding the facts leading to the Nazi's flight to Scotland.

What *was* the truth? What could be so shocking that the public mustn't know? Philip thought that the public should be privy to everything the government planned behind closed doors. What was the point of having a government if it didn't serve the needs of the people? To hell with the Official Secrets Act! It was just a cover for subterfuge.

"Tom," Philip said to the barman when he came on duty in the afternoon, "you remember that officer I had drinks with the other evening?

"The leftenant? Came in here regular as clockwork. Liked his nip or two in the evening."

"Have you heard anything about him? It seems he's no longer posted up the mountain."

"I'm not surprised," Tom said. He looked at Philip with steely eyes. "He was a bit too loose with his lips after his second or third gin. Not surprised a'tall."

"But on such short notice?"

" 'Twas long overdue. If you don't mind a bit of advice," Tom said, "I'd disregard most of what he said the other night. There's no truth to any of it. Just a man with too much to drink talking out of turn."

Philip turned away and walked to the other end of the bar. Was the bartender in on it too? Or was he mad himself? He and Rudolf Hess. Two loony birds lost in the clouds, ready to crash to earth if they didn't watch where they were going.

CHAPTER FIFTEEN

"I MUST PROTEST, Doctor Guthrie," Hess said. "You have deliberately deceived me."

"How so?"

"After our last visit I was led to believe I could return to my homeland."

"I made you no such promises."

"You have been interrogating me like a common prisoner of war," Hess said. "Do you deny it? I demand to be treated like a visiting head of state."

Sir John Simon studied Hess from across the room. They stood in the living room of Hess's quarters, two statesmen fencing with each other. The man was clearly a fanatic, that much was certain. But did that in and of itself make him mad? Did it diminish him as an adversary? He had managed to extract little or nothing from Hess the last time he visited. Simon's so-called "sugar-coated approach," as he had described it to Churchill, had been unsuccessful. Perhaps it was time to change his tactics.

"Understand your position, Herr Hess," Simon said. "You are not, I repeat, *not* a visiting head of state. Heads of state do not parachute uninvited onto foreign soil. You are an international embarrassment—to your own nation as well as mine. Is that quite clear?"

Hess hesitated a long moment, then glared defiantly at Simon.

"All that is clear to me, Doctor Guthrie," Hess said, "is that I have nothing to say to you, no information to supply to you other than the message I have already delivered, until I have been given my freedom to return. I am not so easily intimidated, sir."

Simon glared back, trying, not altogether successfully, to hide the exasperation in his eyes. They had arrived at another impasse. Rudolf Hess was not going to be easy to crack. Perhaps he needed more time to reconsider. A few more weeks in isolation might go a long way in weakening his resolve.

AT HIS HEADQUARTERS in the Wolf's Lair, Hitler studied the report from the field. The German army had crossed the frontier into Russia in three long columns. Resistance had been spotty, and the well-trained troops of the Reich had had little difficulty grinding the Russians into the soil, pushing them back away from their borders. Despite opposition from his generals—those damned dilettantes again—Hitler had ordered the cities destroyed, the wounded massacred, the survivors taken to slave camps.

The German generals, who claimed to believe in following the accepted rules of warfare, had accused the Führer of failing to understand them properly. What they soon learned was that Hitler understood the rules all too well—and he was replacing them with his own. This was to be a quick war. He would be the conqueror of European Russia before Christmas, and to accomplish that he had to fight a war of total annihilation.

For the Russian campaign, Adolf Hitler had moved his headquarters to the forest of East Prussia. His hut was nearly as small as the dingy garrets he had occupied as a starving artist in Vienna. The furniture was spartan—a table for a desk, four straight-back wooden chairs, an old rug, oak paneling on the walls, a painting of Frederick the Great by Anton Graff to remind him of his sacred mission.

Until now Hitler had allowed his generals to conduct the war in Europe. From this moment on he would be the commander of German forces, and his generals would follow his orders as he directed their operations in remote outposts from northern Norway to the islands of Greece. At his insistence, the Wolf's Lair—as he called his new home—was to be free of music, opera and the presence of beautiful women. His sole pleasure would be the orchestration of the movements of the great German armies.

Behind the Führer's back the generals described the Wolf's Lair as a cross between a cloister and a concentration camp. The center of operations stood in the middle of a complex of checkpoints, mine fields and lookout posts. Three rings of barbed wire encircled the hut, and only a few of Hitler's most trusted aides were permitted to enter the inner circle. A radio station, telephone exchange, railroad, mess hall and accommodations for his guards were built outside the outer ring. Camouflage netting covered the buildings and railroad siding.

Hitler was totally isolated from the world—just as he had been in his tormented youth. But now, barricaded in the quiet, lonely and damp Prussian forest, he had at his disposal the power to destroy the entire civilized world.

As troops of the German Reich advanced further into Russia, supply problems began to mount and enemy resistance grew fiercer. Hitler ordered the armies to push ahead, promising them reinforcements from the panzer and armor divisions. He directed Army Group North to march full speed ahead toward Leningrad. Army Group Center was to set up a defensive perimeter and Army Group South was to seize the Crimea and the industrial and coal-producing regions of the Donets Basin, and to cut off Russian oil supply from the Caucasus.

His generals, with the exception of Paulus, argued against this strategy. They sent missives from the battlefield to the Wolf's Lair, stating that the conquest of Moscow was by far the most serious objective of the campaign. All else paled by comparison. Destroy Moscow, the head and heartbeat of Russia, and the rest of the country would die with it. Hitler resisted their advice, maintaining that Moscow would fall like an overripe plum into his hand once they captured Kiev and Leningrad.

The generals were stunned by Hitler's intransigence. General Heinz Guderian, leader of the panzer forces, took the extraordinary measure of leaving the field of action and flying to Hitler's Prussian hideaway to confront the Führer directly. Expecting the worst, he was surprised to find the Führer in a jovial mood when he arrived. Hitler heard him out patiently, with that twisted smile on his lips and not a trace of humor in his eyes.

"Do you think the troops are in condition to make a great effort—a superhuman effort—to end the war before winter?" Hitler asked.

"If they are given a major objective, the importance of which is apparent to every soldier, the answer is yes," Guderian said.

"You mean Moscow, of course," said Hitler.

"That is my opinion and the opinion of the other generals." Guderian went on to repeat his earlier arguments, more forcefully now that Hitler seemed receptive to them. Again the Führer allowed him to speak without interruption. Hitler smiled and nodded when Guderian was through, then told him to return to the battlefield at once. Guderian flew back, warmed by the glow of his success. The Führer had finally acquiesced to logic and reason.

But when Guderian arrived back at the front, he was shocked to learn that Hitler had issued an order in his absence commanding him to hurl the bulk of his forces against Chernigov in the south, not Moscow in the north. Hitler's major objective was unchanged. He would conquer Kiev first, then Leningrad—which he insisted on referring to as St. Petersburg—before he entered Moscow. Apparently he had never seriously considered Guderian's arguments.

His true intentions were carefully outlined in the directive. They could not have been more explicit—or more chilling:

"Petersburg is to be razed to the ground. There is no point in the continued existence of this vast settlement after the defeat of Soviet Russia.

"The original request by the navy that the wharf, harbor and other installations of naval importance should be spared has been noted by the High Command of the Armed Forces, but has to be refused in view of the basic policy in regard to Petersburg.

"It is intended that the city be surrounded and then razed by a general artillery barrage and by continuous air bombardment. Individual surrenders are unacceptable, because we cannot and do not wish to deal with the problem of quartering and feeding the population. We, for our part, have no interest in preserving any section of the population in the course of this war for Germany's survival."

Not since the days of Genghis Khan and Timur lane had one man attempted to annihilate entire cities on such a scale.

The generals studied the directive with foreboding. Their orders were explicit. Their only course was to follow them— or defy the Führer and risk being shot for treason.

RUDOLF HESS LOVED his radio. It was his only link to the outside world, aside from the silly fat officer who had been assigned to drive him around and take walks with him in the woods. But he had abruptly disappeared. The man wasn't such good company anyway, just a bourgeois lout who must have been drafted into the officer ranks because of Britain's manpower shortage.

When he wasn't listening to the radio or visiting the local ruins, Hess devoured the books that were available from the infirmary library and listened to Mozart and Brahms on the Victrola. He had enjoyed his occasional conversations with the psychiatrist whose flat he was occupying, until he found out from Leftenant Wilkins that the man was a Jew.

"Keep your Jewish face out of my apartment, out of my presence," he said the next time the doctor visited him.

While life on the estate in Wales was pleasant enough, Hess was anxious to return to his homeland. The Führer needed him at the front.

"You're being treated well, I presume?" John Simon said during a visit in late June.

"I have no complaints about my treatment, Doctor Guthrie, but as I've told you I'm anxious to go home. This is a critical juncture in the war. I should be at the front."

"Yes, yes." Simon walked over to the balcony and gazed out toward the hills and soft green mountains on the horizon. He was growing tired of the pretense, tired of vacillating between intimidation and the forced affability that masked his contempt. "In due time, of course. We've got to be extremely careful how we handle the situation."

"I heard news of the Russian campaign on the wireless. All is going as planned, is it not? The war should be over before winter—eight weeks, ten weeks at the most."

Simon turned toward him abruptly. Hess was staring at him anxiously, the damp eyes holding his own.

"If only that were certain," Simon said. "Reports are spotty—and contradictory. We hear one thing from your country and quite another from the Russians. It's a question of sorting it all out."

"Surely you don't think the Russians are capable of stopping the forces of the Wehrmacht. Their troops are demoralized, their tanks and artillery old and badly maintained. Already we've taken Vilna, Riga and Lithuania."

"You're right. Perhaps in another week or two when the eventual outcome is clearer, when British intelligence informs us—"

"Hah!"

"You find that amusing?"

"British intelligence!" Hess said. "A contradiction in terms. British intelligence is our best ally. Did you know that Göring instructs his pilots not to bomb SIS headquarters in London in order not to interrupt our stream of information?"

"I see you've adopted a British sense of humor during your visit," Simon said. The extra weeks of isolation seemed to have loosened Hess's tongue a bit.

"It's true. There are more Bolsheviks in your intelligence service than in Moscow. Someday, when the war is over, I'll be happy to give you an accounting of all the turncoats we've uncovered."

Simon was about to deny it, then decided that to do so would be foolish. He and Churchill had suspected for months that SIS was riddled with pinkos. What they did not know was that the Gerries were onto them as well. If they had truly succeeded in monitoring English communications with Moscow, his plan of supplying Russia with arms could be in jeopardy.

"We're well aware that intelligence is filled with communist sympathizers," Simon said. "What you need to determine is which are genuine and which are disseminating bogus information for your own spies to pass on to the Führer."

"Of course!" Hess laughed out loud. "I always enjoy your visits, Doctor Guthrie. I don't have any other opportunity for intelligent conversation here. It's good to exchange views with a worthy adversary."

"Indeed." Simon stared at Hess for a long moment, permitting a smile to soften his face. "Meanwhile, you've got everything you need here. Books, music, the flower garden. I see you sketch too."

Simon picked up a notepad partially filled with drawings Hess had made of the surrounding hills, the garden, a bowl of fruit, a vase.

"Not very well," Hess said. "My talents, such as they are, are more literary than visual."

Simon said nothing, but continued to study the sketches as though searching for a clue to the workings of Hess's mind. The man obviously had a certain taste for music and art, limited though it was, and yet was just as obviously a fanatical devotee of Hitler's violent credo.

"I have no complaints about my treatment," Hess said, "but I must return to the front. Why the delay? Why am I being kept here against my will when I've asked repeatedly to be sent home?"

Simon stared at Hess, looked back at the sketches, then up at Hess again. How could he possibly fail to understand the nature of his predicament?

"Herr Hess, you must realize how sensitive this situation is. My government has to avoid any appearance of collusion at all costs. If the Russians found out, if our other allies . . ."

"But it's immaterial once Russia is defeated. When we achieve our goals in the east it will amount to a fait accompli. France, the United States, the entire world have no alternative but to accept the balance of power between our countries."

"And if you fail?"

"Impossible. Neither one of us can let that happen. If the Russians prevail, my dear Doctor Guthrie, then Russia and America will be the new world powers, and both England and Germany will be their satellites. Surely you can see that."

Hess was right. This was a possibility that Simon and the prime minister had discussed at length. All the more reason why it was so important to orchestrate this Russian campaign just so—to prolong the conflict until both sides were fully exhausted. Then England would have the opportunity to negotiate an equal partnership with the Americans afterward. A quick and decisive victory for either Stalin or Hitler would result in a diminished role for Britain, despite Hess's assurances.

"So why not join with us now?" Hess said, encouraged by Simon's silence. "Why maintain this ludicrous veil of secrecy? Let's achieve our mutual goal together openly instead of continuing a deception that can only haunt you later on."

Hess's logic was impeccable—once you accepted his premise that Hitler could be trusted to leave Britain in peace after the conquest of Soviet Russia. But no one save the most diehard Germanophiles—Windsor, Hamilton and their ilk—believed that. It was just a question of time before the Führer turned his insatiable hunger for new conquests to England.

"That's out of the question," Simon said. "We have no choice but to hedge our bets. After Germany has succeeded in eradicating Bolshevism—with our help—then we can begin a new stage in our negotiations. Until then, everything hangs in the balance."

"Am I to understand, then, that you're going to detain me until winter before releasing me?"

"Perhaps you'd be in greater danger in Germany than you are here. Have you thought of that?"

"What are you suggesting?" There was a glint of fear in Hess's eyes.

"Nothing. Just a thought."

"My wife? She is all right?"

"So far as we know."

"Have there been threats to her safety? To mine?"

"None we're aware of," Simon said.

"Then why must I wait until winter to be released?"

"You've told me yourself," Simon said, "that you expect Moscow to fall in six or eight weeks. That's not too long to wait, is it? You're treated well, you've all the comforts you need."

"But I am a prisoner nonetheless."

"A guest, Herr Hess. A guest of an awkward host, if you like, whose discomfort was brought about by your unfortunate method of arrival on our shores. The situation being highly sensitive, we have to bear with each other—for the moment, at least—until the outcome of the Russian campaign is a bit clearer."

The two men studied each other in silence for several moments. Simon was courteous, but implacable. Hess's fate was determined until early winter at the earliest. Outrageous it might be, but the Deputy Führer of the Third Reich was in fact a prisoner of the British government.

CHAPTER SIXTEEN

July 1941

A LOW SKY hung over Liverpool, as soiled and gray as dirty laundry. It matched perfectly the squalor of the city, the gritty drab streets, the long lines of bleak row houses that stretched down Threadneedle to the pier.

Philip Renfield picked his way down the street, looking for number forty-eight. He wore a heavy wool muffler over his jacket to protect his throat and chest from the unseasonable chill and the dampness. Each building was indistinguishable from the next, gray and homely, the grime of a hundred years caked into the stone. An occasional potted geranium on a window ledge provided the only color. Wash hung limply on sagging lines; sheets, socks and undergarments as gray as the street, as colorless as the passing faces on the sidewalk.

Philip paused halfway down the street, looking up to read the faded numbers above the doorway. There was forty-eight, the eight leaning over on its side. Children's toys, a bag of garbage and empty beer bottles littered the stoop. The stench of dog droppings fouled the air, along with the odor of human urine. He mounted the stairs and looked for the roster of tenants in the lobby, but most of the names were missing or obscured. Visiting strangers rarely came for any other reason than to collect unpaid bills.

He entered the hallway and knocked on the first door on the right. A moment passed, then another.

He rapped again and this time a woman's voice called out, "I 'eard you the first time. What is it you want?"

"I'm looking for Leftenant Harry Wilkins."

"And who are you?"

"A friend. I knew him when we were posted down in Wales together. He gave me his address but I don't know what flat he's in."

"Second-floor rear, for all the good it'll do you. He ain't been seen around here in ages."

Philip continued up the stairway to the second landing and walked toward the rear. A naked lightbulb dangled from an overhead cord, casting a dim glow that did not quite reach into the corners. The door to the back apartment was slightly ajar, which surprised him. Just as he was about to knock, it opened wide to reveal a young woman who clutched her chest when she saw him standing there.

"Oh! You gave me a start. What are you doing there?"

"I'm sorry, I was about to knock. I'm Charles Rogers, a friend of Harry Wilkins. I stopped by to visit him."

She stared at him for a long moment, studying his face with searching eyes.

"A friend of Harry's?" she said.

"Yes. Met him down in Wales when he was posted at Monmouthshire. Can I come in? I'd like to ask you a few questions."

"Well, I was about to take his nibs for a stroll." She motioned toward a toddler strapped into a stroller, dressed to go out.

"You have news of Harry, you say?" She backed into the flat and he followed after her. She stood in the middle of the tiny living room staring at him. There was clutter everywhere—toys, clothing, too much cheap furniture crowded into too small a space.

"What did you say your name was?"

"Charles. Charles Rogers."

"Never heard Harry mention you."

"I haven't known him long. Met him a week ago in Wales, in a pub near his base."

"Sounds like Harry, all right. He's always been keen on his pubs."

"And your name is?"

"Jenny. I'm not surprised you don't know it. Most friends of Harry don't even know he's married."

Philip smiled at the toddler, who gurgled and pumped his fists, then looked back at Jenny. She was pretty, though plain at first glance, a spray of freckles across her nose, her light brown hair pulled back into a ponytail. She would be quite attractive with better clothes, a touch of color in her cheeks, a looser hairstyle.

"What is it you want from me, then?" she said.

"I didn't mean to barge in on you like this, but it's rather important. Do you mind?" He gestured toward the sofa across the room.

"Don't suppose a few minutes more or less will matter. There's not much to do these days anyway. Come, love."

She reached down to her son and unbuttoned his jacket, then undid her own and took it off. Her figure was quite trim without the outer garment. High breasts, rounded hips and nicely tapered legs with slender ankles. Philip unwound his scarf and set it on the coffee table.

"Can I get you some tea, then?"

"If it's not any trouble."

"That's one thing I'm well supplied with. Not much else in the larder, but plenty of Earl Gray."

She filled the kettle and put it on the gas stove in the kitchenette, then sat down across from him to wait for the whistle.

"So tell me, Mr.—"

"Charles, please."

"Charles. Nothing's happened to Harry, has it? He's all right?"

"Oh yes, it's nothing like that. I'm a solicitor and I was down in Wales on holiday when I ran into him at the hotel I was staying in. We chatted in the pub most of the evening, then made plans to do it again the following night. Only he never showed. When I called the base they told me he was no longer there—which I found odd. No advance warning or anything."

"That *is* odd." The whistle went off on the stove and she got up to pour the tea. The toddler stumbled across the room, half walking, half falling, and grabbed onto Philip's leg, saliva running down his chin.

"Don't mind him," Jenny said. She set the teapot on the table to brew. "Not often he sees a man around here. He's that excited."

Philip looked at the boy, searching for a resemblance. Women always seemed to find one, but to Philip he looked like any young kid—fat, jowly, blubbery—a miniature Winston Churchill.

"Harry did talk about you," Philip lied. "He mentioned you and the little one, I just forgot your names. Do you mind?" He offered her his pack of cigarettes, and she took one with thanks. His cough erupted as soon as he inhaled from his own, and the boy started to wail.

"Did he really?" she said. "Talk about us, I mean?"

"He did, yes. Tell me, when's the last you heard from him?"

"A letter three weeks ago, and that was it. He's not much for keeping in touch, is Harry. I'm surprised he even gave you our address."

Philip hesitated a moment, then said, "He didn't. I got it from the war office files when I found out he was gone. A letter, you say? Do you still have it?"

"Suppose I do. It's not often I hear from him. I think I'd fall down stone dead if he sent a pound or two to feed his son, let alone me."

"If it's not too much of an imposition, do you suppose I could see it? The letter?"

She turned away and blew out smoke, then looked at him with a playful smile.

"Keen on reading other people's love notes, are you?" she said.

"I'm sorry. I didn't mean to . . ."

"That's all right. The only time Harry turns mushy is when he comes home with a snootful and feels like a bit of skirt. Mostly he's just full of himself. Hold on a minute while I fetch it."

Philip was touched by her playful air, tinged with bitterness as it was. He watched her walk across the room to a stack of papers in the kitchen area, observed the movement of thigh beneath the skirt.

"I did keep it, after all," she said. "You're in luck."

She handed him the letter and sat back down across from him. She motioned toward his cigarettes.

"Do you mind?" she said.

"Not at all. Help yourself. Here, keep the pack, I've got more than I need in my hotel."

Philip read the handwritten letter, looking for anything at all to help him sort out the random threads:

Jenny dear,

I know I've been a bit of a shit, not writing or calling like I should. I hope you and little Harry are doing fine, give him my love, all right? Do you have enough to eat? I've been meaning to send along a few nicker to help you out, and I promise I will if not the next payday then the one after for sure. A serviceman's pay doesn't go very far, I can tell you that.

I am doing just fine so don't worry your pretty head about me, although my new assignment in the booby hatch is enough to drive anyone barmy, especially a bloke like me who's been in the thick of it and all.

But I'm onto something top secret here—a secret duty I can't talk to anyone about—not even you. I can tell you I'm dealing with some very top brass though—high level stuff. I don't mind telling you we're fighting the wrong enemy. Ought to be helping the Gerries clear the world of Bolshies instead of the other way around. That's how I see it anyway.

That's all for now, love. I've been blabbing on too long already. Duty calls me as they say. I will write again soon I promise. And send a few bob for you and the nipper when I can spare it.

Yours,

Harry

Philip read the letter twice, then placed it on the coffee table. Jenny blew smoke out in a stream across the room.

"Touching little love note, isn't it?" she said.

Philip looked up at her. There was a tightness about her eyes, as if she were holding back tears.

"How did you get . . . get . . ."

"Get mixed up with the silly ass?" she said.

"Well, yes, I suppose that is what I meant." He could not help chuckling.

"The usual way. Met him in a pub one night, both of us stiff as sheets. In ordinary times I wouldn't have given him five minutes I don't think. I like my men on the thin side."

She looked at Philip a moment without smiling. He was more than a bit on the thin side.

"Women can't be choosy these days," she said, "what with half the young men in the country getting their legs blown away. Nothing but old codgers and nutters left to choose from. Oops, sorry."

"About what?"

"I didn't mean you. I wouldn't consider you old or . . . or . . ."

"Or daft," he said. They both laughed nervously at that. Philip had ten to twelve years on her at least. "I don't think of myself as old, either. The daft part I'm not sure about."

"Anyway," she said, "one thing led to another and before you could count to ten, I was in a motherly way as they say. Harry almost flipped. The last thing that bugger wanted to be was a father."

She looked at her son.

"I'm grateful the little one doesn't understand a word of English yet—do you, love?"

"But he married you anyway?"

"Married! Hah! That's what we told the old bitch downstairs so she'd let us this flat, frightful as it is. I wouldn't go to see Harry's butcher, so he agreed to fix us up here, paid the owner a few months down, and then . . . it's off to the National Service."

"He enlisted?"

She extracted another cigarette from his packet without asking and put it to her lips. Philip reached across and lit it for her.

"Enlisted, yes. He was exempt before that, feet flatter than flounders. Guess he decided he'd rather take his chances fighting wogs than making a go of it here. Don't blame him really. It's not very pretty. But it puts us in a devilish fix."

"I can't say I'm surprised," Philip said. "That sounds pretty much like the man I met in Wales."

"So that's my life story—touching, isn't it? What I don't understand is why you're so keen on tracking him down yourself. Doesn't sound as though you're too fond of him either."

Philip looked at her and smiled. Her eyes were bright, but the tears were gone. There was an intelligence there he hadn't seen before. How much could he tell her? How much should he?

"I mentioned before I was a solicitor on holiday when I ran into your . . . when I ran into Harry. That's not quite true, but I can't go into all the details. . . ."

"Top secret, like Harry's assignment?"

He looked sharply at her but she was smiling, playing with him.

"Sorry," she said.

"Yes, well, I see your point, all this subterfuge and so on. But it is rather sensitive. When Harry didn't return the next night I began to suspect . . . well, foul play. There's just no logical explanation for his disappearing from the base like that."

"But what on earth—"

"Believe me when I tell you the less you know about this, the better. But Harry knew something that was best kept to himself. He was sworn to secrecy. It's part of his job. Only—"

"Only Harry's not very good at keeping secrets," she said. "Buy him a round or two and he'll flap his gums for hours if you let him. Loves to pump himself up bigger than he is."

"This time his mouth may've gotten him into more trouble than he needed. I don't know. It doesn't add up. He disappears on the spur of the moment, doesn't call you, the war office won't say where he is . . ."

"And what about you? If there is foul play, as you said, where does that leave you? You were the last one . . . I mean . . ."

"The last one he talked to," Philip said. "I know, I've already thought of that. I've been warned before to keep my nose away from where it doesn't belong, but I never seem to learn."

She looked at him, then frowned without replying.

"I didn't mean to drag you into this, I really didn't. I just thought—"

"I've a right to know. I'm glad you told me."

"I'd better get back to my hotel," he said. "I've got some phone calls to make, leads to follow up on."

"You will—I mean, if it's not too much trouble—"

"I'll keep you posted. As soon as I learn anything at all."

"I'd like that," she said.

So would I, he thought. So would I. He got up to go.

"Good luck," she said.

"Careful is better. When you're careful you make your own good luck."

Little Harry gurgled and fell down on his rump. He smiled and a strong odor filled the air.

"Seems as though you've a job of your own to tend to," Philip said.

"Keeps me busy, he does. If I'm not sticking food in his mouth I'm wiping his bottom."

Philip smiled and then he was gone. He could feel Jenny watching him go down the stairwell, listening to his footsteps until they faded into silence.

CHAPTER SEVENTEEN

August 1941

Hᴉᴛʟᴇʀ's ʜᴇᴀʟᴛʜ ᴡᴀs deteriorating rapidly. At least he felt it was. This damned Prussian swamp. This rotten weather. The food. If it wasn't diarrhea or nausea, it was aching joints and limbs. He was shivering with cold one minute, boiling with heat the next. Already he was up to a 150 anti-gas pills a week, plus ten injections of a strong sulfonamide to fight bacterial infections. He had started to worry about his heart too. Damn Guderian and Blumentritt. Damn all the generals. All they did was cause him grief, resist his orders, get his armies bogged down outside Leningrad instead of forging ahead as he commanded.

Now he had to deal with that pompous fool Mussolini as well. What good was his support? What good were his troops—undisciplined ragamuffins with no heart for combat. The fat buffoon was losing control. He was an embarrassment to the Reich. Supposedly he had contracted syphilis on top of everything else. So typical of his race.

The Führer met the Duce without ceremony at the local

railroad station. The weather was overcast again, and the dim light of the forest added to the general gloom. Hitler escorted him at once to the tiny room at the heart of the Wolf's Lair.

When last they met, Mussolini had been hale and robust, the very picture of the strutting Latin peacock. Today he was grayer and thinner, as if he had aged and diminished inside his bulky green-gray uniform. Mussolini stared around at Hitler's quarters with unconcealed horror. *This* was where the conqueror of Europe, the supreme commander of the Third Reich, ruled over his empire? Such a tiny, stifling room more appropriate for a hermit than a powerful dictator.

Hitler wasted no time in pleasantries. With both their translators standing at attention, staring malevolently at each other as though reflecting the truculence of their masters, Hitler began.

"The campaign in the east is virtually over," he said, pacing back and forth across the room while Mussolini sat and watched. Sweat ran down the Italian's face and neck, soaking the collar of his uniform. The heat was suffocating, but Hitler did not seem to feel it.

"Troops of the Reich are already outside Leningrad, ready to strike," he said. "And Moscow will be ours by October."

Mussolini glowered as he listened to the smaller man's tirade, thrusting his famous chin forward, waiting for an opening. The combination of heat and bombast began to dull the Duce's senses. His eyelids drooped, his lips went slack. If Hitler noticed he did not comment. From time to time Mussolini's head jerked up, his senses registered sentences and phrases, fragments of the diatribe, then he nodded off again.

". . . England is finished. Churchill thinks the Americans will save him. Roosevelt is surrounded by Jews, they are urging him into the war, but by the time he is ready, Moscow will be a lake and England will be annexed by the Reich."

After what seemed like hours, the Führer was finished and

he collapsed into his chair, his eyes dull with spent rage. Mussolini perked up from his half-slumber, rose to his feet and stared down at the exhausted Führer, his eyes now shining with an intensity of their own.

Hitler looked up in amazement at the dictator, who now marched back and forth across the narrow room, five steps this way, five steps that way, his jaw thrust out, his right hand inside his uniform Napoleon-style. For forty-five minutes, Hitler listened dumbly as Mussolini lectured him on the glories of ancient Rome, the military strategies and conquests of Trajan and Caesar, the courage of the Roman legions in the face of greater numbers of enemies—all of it striking Hitler as an indirect criticism of his conduct of the war on the eastern front. Furious—and momentarily speechless—the Führer picked up the phone when the Duce concluded his address and demanded that food be brought to them immediately. Lunch. It was already four o'clock in the afternoon.

Mussolini, invigorated by his own performance, smacked his lips in anticipation of a meal. A feast for the two most powerful men in Europe—no, the world. Perhaps some meat, a bottle of wine, a little brandy.

But when the sergeant arrived with a tray of food, Mussolini's spirits plummeted again. This was a meal? Steamed vegetables, a boiled potato for each of them and a handful of cream cakes. And what was that dishwater he was expected to wash it down with? Tepid tea diluted with canned milk. It looked as gray as the day outside, as dreary as this damp, impossible forest the Führer had summoned him to.

Amazingly, the Führer's mood changed for the better after they ate. The mood swing was dramatic. He smiled, faced his guest and asked him directly for additional Italian support in the east for the first time that day.

"The Italian army, the entire people, are behind you one hundred percent," Mussolini said. "I am ready on a moment's notice to send reinforcements to the Russian front. Just say the word."

Hitler was positively beaming.

"Of course Franco is a fool," Mussolini said. "He is untrustworthy, interested only in his own survival. England lacks the will to fight and the Americans will stay out of it—rest assured of that."

This, of course, was exactly what Hitler wanted to hear. Mussolini failed to add that he firmly believed Russia was far better prepared than Hitler realized. England was not defeated, her bombs were falling everywhere, and Churchill was merely buying time to rebuild his forces. Roosevelt was inching closer to war by the minute. The Russian campaign would not be over by winter. It would keep the Germans occupied for months, maybe years. Italian morale was low, and without German support the Allies would overrun the peninsula with little resistance. Mussolini himself was sicker than he cared to admit. Sick and dispirited. In his opinion, Hitler was blundering badly. He would not heed the advice of his own generals—and certainly would not listen to Mussolini.

"When this is all over, my friend," Hitler said, "I look forward to visiting you in Italy."

"It would be my honor. I will personally escort you around Florence. It is a city unsurpassed by any other for its art and its natural beauty. Superior even to Paris."

Hitler smiled. At least the Italian dictator would support his vision, even if his own generals would not.

LATER IN THE week, despite Mussolini's eagerness to leave, he flew at the Führer's request to the Russian front. At General von Rundstedt's headquarters at Uman in the Ukraine, surrounded by a disillusioned phalanx consisting of German

and Italian soldiers, the two dictators and General von Rundstedt lunched in the open air together. Hitler talked, Mussolini nodded halfheartedly in agreement, and von Rundstedt
did his best to conceal his opposition to the Führer's grand
plan. After lunch, Hitler inspected the troops while the German general and the Fascist leader were left to their own
devices—von Rundstedt eyeing the Duce with open contempt, Mussolini staring down his nose at the German in an
attempt to assert his higher rank.

During their return trip to the Prussian forest Mussolini
decided to have some fun. Aware that Hitler was terrified of
airplanes and always insisted on his personal pilot and chauf-
feur, Hans Baur, transporting him wherever he went, and
looking for a way to extract some revenge for his week of
unrelieved misery in Hitler's company, Mussolini jumped up
suddenly during the flight, entered the cockpit and told Baur
to step aside while he took over the controls.

An accomplished pilot, Mussolini climbed, then dove, and
put the aircraft through its paces. Hitler remained riveted to
his seat, gripping the armrests. Not once during the entire
flight did he take his eyes from the back of Mussolini's head.
He was still rigid with barely controlled hysteria as the Italian
leader swooped in for a landing. When the ordeal was over,
Hitler jumped to his feet and rushed forward.

"My congratulations," he said, his lips white. "A virtuoso
performance."

Mussolini accepted the accolade with delight. It was the
most fun he had had in a week, so much fun in fact that he
included the episode in his communiqué describing their
journey.

SIR JOHN SIMON stared at the antics on the screen, fidgeting
nervously. Churchill sat beside him, smoking another of his

abominable cigars and sipping his fifth brandy of the evening. John Simon was counting.

There were times when the prime minister infuriated him, and this was one of them. There was something positively infantile about the man. Simon had rushed over to deliver urgent news. Not only had Winston made him wait, he'd insisted that Simon sit through a Marx Brothers comedy with him. The Marx Brothers! Idiocy! A war was raging, important matters needed to be discussed, and Churchill insisted it could all wait until he finished viewing this inane American film on his private screen for perhaps the sixth or seventh time.

The film finally ended. The lights went up and Simon looked over to see the prime minister mopping tears from his eyes and brandy from his chin.

"I tell you, John," Churchill said, "it does the soul good. Nobody makes me laugh the way they do." His wattles jiggled, his entire body shook. "Well, W. C. Fields, perhaps."

"Indeed."

"Oh, do loosen up, will you? Here, have another spot of brandy."

He filled Simon's glass nearly to the top. Simon had no intention of drinking it, but no matter—Churchill would down it himself after he left.

He got up, and Simon followed him into the study, marveling at his purposeful gait—the man seemed able to will himself back to sobriety whenever the need arose. Many had judged him on appearances in the past, and many had been outwitted as a result.

The prime minister settled into his favorite chair and rekindled his cigar. Simon sat nearby, his untouched brandy in hand. He waited patiently while Churchill studied the glowing ash until he was content it was properly lit.

"So, John," he said, "what do you have for me? I assume it's this Hess business again."

"Hess isn't the problem at the moment. Not that he isn't ripping mad because we won't let him go back to his beloved Fatherland, but there's not much he can do about it. If he knew what was in store for him he wouldn't be so eager to return. It's this Renfield chap who concerns me."

"The reporter?"

"The one who broke the story, yes."

"I thought we had him bottled up," Churchill said.

"So far as our own media is concerned. But he's not content to let it lie. He's poking around where he doesn't belong, and I'm certain he suspects the deception. Worse, I'm afraid it's just a question of time before he goes to the foreign press with it."

"What harm can that do? It's all surmise on his part. He doesn't know anything for certain, does he?"

"We can't be sure he won't find out," Simon said. How could Churchill be so cavalier about it? The potential damage was enormous.

"Well, it *is* wartime, John," Churchill said. "Official secrets and all that. Can't we put him in protective custody?"

"I've thought of that," Simon said, "but it may not be so easy. What if he's in on this with someone else?"

"What do you mean?"

"*Someone* must be financing this quest of his. If that's the case, I think we should know who it is."

"I see what you mean." Churchill studied his cigar. "How far has he gone?"

"All the way to the driver's wife," Simon said. "He's tracked her down in Liverpool."

Winston looked up. "No harm in that, surely. She can't tell him anything of value, can she?"

"No." Simon bit the word off, not bothering to hide his annoyance. Why was Churchill playing dumb, forcing him to state the obvious? "She doesn't know anything herself. But she's a link to Wilkins, his family, his whereabouts if he tries to contact any of them."

"Ah yes." Churchill puffed lightly on the end of his cigar. "And just where is the chatty leftenant now?"

How many times did he have to be told?

"Back in North Africa," Simon said.

"Out of harm's way?"

"Yes. Well, not exactly. His division is right in the thick of it. Anything could happen, anything at all. There are shells falling everywhere, bullets flying all around. T'would be a pity if one of them found him."

"My thoughts exactly," said Churchill.

CHAPTER EIGHTEEN

Rudolf Hess sunk his garden tool into the earth, settled the last of the tulip bulbs into the hole, then patted the dirt down lightly around it. He stood up and pushed his palms against his lower back to work out the stiffness. The garden had been his sole outdoor activity for weeks, his only exercise since he had been confined to the grounds around his flat. He rose early, took his breakfast alone, then went out into the garden to work until lunchtime. The afternoons were ordinarily spent writing in his journal, listening to music or radio news, and sketching the surrounding mountains from his patio.

Had there been any question up until now as to whether he was a prisoner of war, it had been answered unequivocally after his last meeting with Dr. Guthrie—if that's who he really was. Hess was beginning to have his doubts. Judging by the man's presence and bearing, the manner in which he conducted himself, the amount of authority he appeared to wield, he was obviously a senior statesman, one of the prime minister's top advisers. That narrowed the field down to two or three, according to German intelligence reports, and Hess had a good idea of who he was. Dr. Guthrie, with his dark, saturnine appearance, had a certain Semitic cast to his features. The fact that the British government would attempt to deceive him like this was proof enough that he was a prisoner—though admittedly a well-treated one. Not an honored guest.

His isolation was virtually total, his only human contact with the old crone who came in to tidy up and bring his meals, his radio the only link with the outside world. As he sat in the living room listening to it one afternoon at the end of August, he was more than a little disturbed by what he heard.

Could it possibly be true, or was it merely British propaganda? According to the reports, Russian resistance had stalled the German advance outside Leningrad. The campaign, it seemed, was beginning to drag on. The Wehrmacht had been hampered by confused strategy in the field as well as mounting supply problems.

Impossible! Unthinkable! How could this be true? The Russians were ill-prepared, their troops poorly trained, their weapons poorly maintained. The German armies, by contrast, had never been readier. Morale was high, equipment was new and efficient, Wehrmacht tanks the best in the world—certainly bigger, more mobile and possessed of greater firepower than anything the Russians had to throw against them.

Hess got up and turned off the radio. Operation Barbarossa had been planned down to the last detail. A lightning attack at dawn. A pincer envelopment of Moscow. A blitzkrieg, swift, brutal—a model of modern military proficiency. What had gone wrong?

If only he could discuss it with the Führer face-to-face. He had no way of contacting Dr. Guthrie; the man visited him when he pleased, then returned to London. The Duke of

Hamilton seemed to have disappeared from the face of the earth. This isolation was intolerable. He needed information. Facts, not lies. Facts about the war, his wife, his family and friends. He would demand to see Guthrie immediately, insist that he be returned to Germany at once. Someone would have to pay for this psychological abuse—for that's what it was—as soon as the war was over.

There was a rap on the door.

"Come in!" he shouted.

The old woman entered with his evening meal.

"I demand to speak to someone in authority here!" He smashed his fist on the table.

The old woman almost dropped her tray. She stood gaping at him from the doorway, not knowing how far to go in, not knowing what to say. Hess dashed across the room at her.

"Don't just stand there, you stupid cow! Get someone! Now! Move!"

The sound that came from her throat was more a gargle than a reply. Hess moved even closer.

"Don't stand there—go get someone! Quickly!"

She wheeled about and ran from the flat, more quickly than she had moved in years.

PHILIP RENFIELD WAS without an official job for the first time in years. Supposedly, he had quit his job at the *Daily Record,* fed up with covering garden club events just as he had when he was a cub reporter. But his real employer was still old man Buchanan, who was financing him—quite unofficially—to unearth the true story of the Hess affair.

There was a virtual news blackout on anything relating to Rudolf Hess, except for official government handouts. Everywhere he turned it was the same. It was as though a great pall had settled over the British press, limiting everything that found its way into print under the abominable Official Secrets Act.

But he knew that something mysterious was going on, something that had nothing to do with national security, something the public ought to know about. And Philip had a good idea what it was.

It was time to move on. So move he did—or at least travel— more and more frequently to Liverpool. The Wilkins thread in the Hess tapestry was all he really had to go on, and it was strong enough to draw him back to that dreary waterfront city to see what else, if anything, he could find out. Leftenant Wilkins was the closest he had been able to get to the real Rudolf Hess.

The second time he visited Jenny, he popped in on her again without notice, straining under the weight of a bag filled with milk, cheese, butter and other staples. She sat down at the kitchen table and cried like an infant, little Harry chiming in with her.

"If I'd known my visit would have this kind of an effect on you, Jenny, I'd have rung you up first," he said.

"Oh, it's not you." She dabbed her eyes, blew her nose, finally smiled up at him. "Not you at all. I'm just not used to such . . . consideration. Look. Little Harry's happy to see you too."

The boy was smiling.

"Let me put the kettle on. How's your cough? I never did thank you the last time, you know."

"Thank me? For what?"

"For lying to me. Harry never mentioned me and the little one like you said, did he?"

Philip looked at the floor.

"The truth, please. Not that it matters, really. I just like to keep accounts straight."

"We had other things to discuss that night. I'm sure if he'd had more time . . ."

"You're sweet," she said. "Sit down over there. I'll fetch some cups."

"Have you heard from Harry since the last time?" asked Philip.

"Not a word. I think he's written us off. It's for the best—there's nothing between us now, except for . . ." She nodded toward the boy.

"Yes, though he should at least be held accountable for his son."

"He's not legal," Jenny said. "Do you have any idea how many girls like me there are in England? Left with children their fathers want no part of?"

"Yes, but still . . ."

"And what of you?" she said. "Are you all right?"

"Aside from the fact that I can't—" He was about to say, "practice my profession freely," then caught himself in time. "I suppose so—everything considered."

Jenny stared at him, frowning deeply. He was obviously not telling her any more than he thought he had to.

He visited her again a few days later, this time bringing canned goods—meat, soups, stew, black market rations. This time she had something to show him. She went into her bedroom, retrieved a newspaper clipping from the drawer of the dresser beside the bed and brought it out to him. It was the weekly list, from the local paper, of the dead and missing in action in the North African campaign. "It's from yesterday," said Jenny.

Philip scanned the list until he reached the bottom. There, three names before the end of the MIAs, was Leftenant Harry Wilkins.

"Dear God!" he said.

"It was the first I'd heard of it," she said.

"They're supposed to notify the next of kin before they publish the names," Philip said.

A toughness he hadn't seen before glinted in her eyes.

"How?" she said. "The filthy bugger never even told the military he had a family here in Liverpool."

CHAPTER NINETEEN

The knock on the door startled Hess. He looked up from his journal and called out, "Who is there?"

"Doctor Guthrie is here to see you," the orderly said through the closed door.

"Just one moment please." Hess hid the notebook in the bottom drawer of the desk, walked over to the center of the room, took a moment to compose himself and said, "Tell him to come in."

He stood erect, stretching himself to his full height, and waited for his visitor to arrive. After several minutes Simon entered the room, unsmiling, his eyes reflecting the sunlight flooding into the room from the balcony behind Hess. Hess studied his guest carefully—the dark brown eyes, the long thin nose, the high bony forehead and receding hairline. He was certain now who Dr. Guthrie really was.

"I'll get right to the point," Simon said. "We've received word that you've been quite . . . agitated, shall we say, of late."

"What do you expect?" Hess said. "I am confined here against my will, isolated for days and weeks at a time with no news—"

"You've got your wireless."

"*Official* news, not propaganda for public consumption."

"Don't speak to me of propaganda," Simon said. "We have a free press in this country, free to report the facts as they occur, which is more than one can say for the state of affairs in your homeland."

"Free, you say?" Hess laughed. "Free within the boundaries of your Official Secrets Act. You call it freedom"—he was about to say "Dr. Guthrie," but stopped himself—"but your idea of freedom is an illusion for the masses. At least we are honest about the state of affairs in Germany. We make no pretenses about such notions of bourgeois democracy that have no basis in reality."

Simon's eyes flashed and his mouth twitched. He measured his response carefully.

"I didn't come here to debate political philosophy with you, Herr Hess. The point is, we can't have you terrorizing the hired help. If it happens again, we'll have no choice but to move you to more remote quarters."

"Perhaps if you were more honest with me," Hess said, "I wouldn't have to resort to such dramatic gestures."

"Honest? What are you referring to?"

"To begin with," Hess said, "there is the question of your true identity. What is your preferred mode of address? Lord chancellor? Or will Sir John do?"

"Sir John will do just fine," Simon said, not missing a beat.

"You needn't have bothered with such transparent deception. How long did you think you could get away with it?"

"Considering the circumstances," Simon said, "the prime minister thought it would be best, and I concurred."

"You are referring to your heritage," Hess said, in the same half-question, half-statement tone the Führer so often used.

"That, plus the ordinary precautions one needs to take in such situations. Had the press known in advance that the lord chancellor was en route to Glasgow, there would have been no avoiding them."

"Such deceptions only reinforce racial stereotypes," Hess said.

Simon returned his adversary's gaze evenly. There was a hint of a playful smile on Hess's lips, but Simon was all business.

"Since you know who I am now," Simon said, "you also know that I have been somewhat critical of the prime minister's adamant stance vis-à-vis your country—notwithstanding my heritage, Herr Hess. Let me hasten to add, however, that my criticism has nothing to do with any misguided ideas about your country and its loathsome policies, but rather with matters of strategic importance."

"Such a position is interpreted in some circles as a mark of weakness, Sir John."

"And in others as a mark of prudence," Simon said.

Hess laughed. "Well put," he said. "History will be the judge of that."

"As it is in all matters," Simon said. "Which brings us full circle to the original question of your mission. Precisely whose idea was it, yours or your Führer's?"

"Now you are interrogating me again," Hess said. "I have a right to remain silent until I know when I shall be permitted to return to the Fatherland. Surely the Führer has demanded that I be sent back home."

"I assure you, you are infinitely safer here than you would be there."

"Do you expect me to believe such lies?"

"You would be executed within days of your return to Germany," Simon said. "Your wife is under house arrest, your adjutant has been incarcerated in Munich, and the entire Haushofer family is being held incommunicado by the Gestapo."

"Lies and more lies!"

"You fail to understand what an acute embarrassment you are to both your own country and mine. You've bungled your mission."

"My mission has been completed, an accommodation has been reached, has it not?"

Hess stared at Simon, who stared back, a glint of disbelief evident in his eyes.

"But, surely," Simon said, searching for words that would make Hess understand, "if the mission had been conducted in secrecy, as was originally planned, no one would be the wiser. But now, with the entire world clamoring for news of your whereabouts and information about your unorthodox arrival—"

"The world be damned!" Rudolf Hess moved from his spot for the first time since Simon's arrival. He strode to the balcony, whirled about and faced Simon. "Who cares what the world thinks? The masses will believe what we want them to. Once Germany has accomplished its goals in the east . . ."

"My dear fellow." Simon did not try to hide the exasperation in his voice. "I've been trying to tell you all along that Germany is nowhere near to accomplishing its goals. It's by no means certain that it ever will."

"Where is your proof?"

"Proof? What sort of proof?"

"Why are you afraid to let me return home and see for myself? To let me speak to my Führer and hear the words from him directly? I am willing to face the consequences you speak of."

"Don't you understand how it would look if we simply allowed you to slip from our grasp in the midst of a war?"

"There you are worrying about world opinion again," Hess said. "Perhaps I overrated you after all."

"This is all quite hopeless, I'm afraid." Simon looked away for the first time since entering Hess's apartment. "Quite hopeless."

Suddenly he turned back, faced Hess directly again and said, "I demand to know when and where this alleged attack of Japan's on the United States is scheduled to occur!"

"I have nothing further to say, Lord Chancellor," Hess said, his voice dripping with sarcasm.

"Nor do I, Herr Deputy Führer!" Simon glared at Hess, then turned on his heel and left the room.

CHAPTER TWENTY

September 1941

Over tea and cream cakes in his cramped quarters at the Wolf's Lair, Adolf Hitler suddenly had a change of heart. Throughout the midday snack he had hardly touched his favorite cakes or sipped from his cup of tea, richly laced with milk. So unlike him, thought Heinrich Heim, one of his aides who had been asked to keep an eye on the Führer by Martin Bormann.

"It is important," Bormann had instructed Heim, "that you take notes on everything he says."

For two weeks now, Heim had been keeping a stack of index cards in his lap on which he surreptitiously wrote down everything the Führer said or did. The other aide present today, Werner Koeppen, had also been jotting down Hitler's mealtime conversations on paper napkins at the behest of Alfred Rosenberg. Neither one knew what the other was up to, nor did they have any way of knowing that both their sets of notes would be published after the war under the title, *Hitler's Tischgespräch*.

Hitler continued to ignore the food, and stared silently at the large map hanging on the wall. His eyes rarely blinked, his gaze never wavered. Heim and Koeppen studied him carefully throughout the long, awkward silence. Finally, Hitler spoke.

"In a few weeks we will be in Moscow." His voice was even. "There's no doubt about it. I'll raze that damned city. The name Moscow will disappear forever."

Hitler stood up and walked over to the map. His back turned to his aides, his eyes riveted on the capital city of Russia, he continued, "Decision consists of not hesitating when an inner conviction commands you to act. Last year I needed great spiritual strength to make the decision to attack Bolshevism. I had to anticipate that Stalin might take the offensive. I had to start without delay, and that wasn't even possible before June. When I think of it, what great luck we had on our side."

The Führer turned around and faced the two aides. His eyes were shining.

"The new world order will be decided after the conquest of Russia. Europe under German rule will be an impregnable fortress, safe from any threat of blockade. All this opens up economic vistas that will incline the most liberal of the western democracies toward our New Order. Right now, the essential thing is to conquer. After that, everything will be a matter of organization."

The Führer once again took his seat and selected a cream cake from the tray. He bit into it with great relish, and stared back at the map on the wall.

"The Slavs were born slaves," he said. "They need a master, and Germany will rule them like the English ruled in India. Complete control with only a handful of men."

Three days later, the capture of Kiev gave Hitler renewed hope. It was the first good news to come out of Russia since the first days of the campaign. Hitler's unbridled optimism in the face of one setback after another and his propensity for uttering statements that sounded more like speeches than normal conversation at odd moments throughout the day were a source of great concern to Rosenberg, Bormann and the rest of the Führer's inner circle. It was as though, in his own mind, he could alter the course of the war by the sheer force of his will alone.

"The capture of Kiev," Hitler remarked at dinner, "means the conquest of the entire Ukraine is now inevitable. It justifies my southern strategy in Russia, despite all the opposition I received from Blumentritt and those other dilettantes. In Kiev alone we took over a hundred and forty-five thousand prisoners. Russia is on the brink of collapse."

Hitler smiled and sipped from his glass of diluted wine. Heim and Koeppen exchanged furtive glances, then looked away, saying nothing. Suddenly, the Führer's smile disappeared and a dark cloud passed over his face.

"Subhumans!" He said. His body shook with revulsion. "Europe will never be free until those monstrous Asiatics are driven back beyond the Urals. Brutes! Bolshevism, czarism, it's all the same to them."

Hitler's mood shifted once again. Anger and revulsion gave way to fear. Fear of the subhuman?

"What is battle?" he asked. Suddenly he was smiling, almost grimacing. "A soldier's first taste of battle is like a woman's first sexual encounter. Each is aggression, but only the first is virtuous. In a day or two the soldier becomes a man. If I myself weren't hardened to the experience, do you think I could have taken on this Herculean mission? This is my burden."

"It is truly heroic," Heim said. Koeppen nodded in agreement, keeping his eyes on the Führer.

"In nineteen fourteen I saw men falling all around me,"

Hitler said. "Thousands of them. Then I learned that life is a struggle and has no other meaning except the preservation of the species."

The following morning, Adolf Hitler ordered an all-out assault on Moscow. Once again his generals resisted, this time because they thought he had waited too long and missed the opportunity for a surprise attack early in the campaign. The weather was already changing over to early winter conditions, they argued. But the Führer prevailed and, in the beginning, his strategy was correct. The Russian high command, completely unprepared for a major offensive this late in the year, was caught by surprise. Sixty-nine German divisions pushed ahead toward Moscow. In the first twenty-four hours alone, Guderian's Second Panzer Group punched its way fifty miles through scattering ranks of Red Army soldiers.

Ecstatic with this renewed momentum, coming as it did on the heels of the victory in Kiev, Hitler took the opportunity to travel in his special train to Berlin. It had been months since he addressed the German people as a nation. Too long. The people needed to hear from their Führer. How could they keep up their morale if their leader was isolated in the forest, brooding over temporary setbacks?

He strode into the Berlin Sportpalast in midafternoon wearing his immaculate white dress uniform, swastikas on the lapels, ribbons running down the left breast, a lightning bolt on each sleeve. His face was aglow. No one would know he was the same man who had been weak with illness in the Prussian forest only days before.

The Sportpalast was a sea of gray and khaki uniforms. Red flags with black swastikas encircled in a field of white hung thickly overhead. Microphones crowded the area in front of the lectern, carrying the Führer's voice to millions of Germans throughout the nation.

"On the morning of June twenty-second," he began in a

strong voice, "the greatest battle in the history of the world began. Since then everything has gone according to plan. Even as I am addressing you today, the enemy is beaten and will never rise again!"

The roar was deafening as it thundered against the walls.

"The invincible German armies have taken two and half million prisoners, captured or destroyed twenty-two thousand pieces of artillery, eighteen thousand tanks, more than fourteen thousand planes. Soldiers of the Reich have advanced a thousand kilometers into Russia and converted more than twenty-five thousand kilometers of railroad track to German use!"

Millions of German civilians sat transfixed by their radios, listening to their Führer's incantations and the thundering of the audience. Few of them had any way of knowing that the mesmerizing depiction of Operation Barbarossa they were hearing bore little resemblance to the facts.

Hitler closed his eyes, looked toward heaven, and pounded the lectern with the flat of his hand.

"Above all, the war in the east is a war of ideologies," he said. "All the best elements in the Reich must now be welded into one indissoluble community. Only then, when the entire German population becomes a single community of sacrifice can we hope and expect that Providence will stand by us in the future. Almighty God never helped a lazy man. Nor does he help a coward!"

The Führer's remarkable performance, which lasted the better part of three hours without interruption, galvanized everyone in the hall as well as his entire radio audience. It was a prodigious feat for a man who had been gripped by despair such a short time before. When he finished, his entire body was drenched in perspiration. He folded his hands under his arms to control the trembling, and smiled broadly at the roaring throng. Despite the inaccuracy of his figures and his fantastic optimism in the face of one setback after another on the eastern front, he knew that he had accomplished beyond his wildest dreams his purpose in addressing the nation. The generals might have been against him, might have thwarted and frustrated him at every turn, yet there was no question but that the entire German people supported him as one.

CHAPTER TWENTY-ONE

Philip's visits to Liverpool, sporadic at first, gradually increased in frequency to a couple of times a week. By the middle of September, he had become aware that his interest in that bleak waterfront city was a bit more complicated than his desire to track down a story. Important as the Hess affair was to him, he realized that he was thinking more and more about Jenny when he was away.

Jenny and her son began to look forward to seeing him as well, and they were also becoming dependent on the groceries and provisions he brought along. The routine they established provided a semblance of stability surrounded by the chaos of war and—in Philip's case—the danger associated with his search for the errant Rudolf Hess.

Now, once again at her apartment, Philip watched as Jenny fed her son. Soon, she put him in his crib. Philip was staring at her when she turned around. They came together, for the first time, without a word. Jenny clung to him with a hunger that heightened his own. He felt her large, soft breasts against his chest, felt her teeth pressing on his. He touched her all over, caressed her back, thighs and buttocks, and her hands roamed freely down his arms, his hips, the front of his trousers until he was ready to burst through them.

Later, in bed, he could not get enough of touching her. The warmth from her body washed over him. He filled her with himself.

Jenny. The sound of her name gave him hope. It was a comforting name for a safe place he could return to and know he would be welcome.

"Jenny, I . . ."

"Hush, love, don't spoil it with words."

She caressed his cheeks and hair, pulled his head down onto her breasts. He could stay there forever, his face buried in her soft flesh, her hands stroking him, his arms wound tightly around her. She was right. Why spoil it with words?

They made love again without speaking, then little Harry awoke from his nap. Jenny smiled, hugged Philip again and got up to tend to her son. Philip rolled onto his back and reached over for his cigarettes.

"Shall I light one for you?" he said.

"Not now. There's a good love," she said to the boy. Philip dragged on his cigarette, covered his mouth to stifle a usual fit of coughing, and watched her ministering to the boy. Should he tell her now, or wait? He had let the deception drag on too long already. The guilt was beginning to get to him.

"This is probably not the best time to tell you," he said, "but it really can't wait. My—my real name is not Charles."

Jenny did not reply, did not look at him. She finished with her son, who now turned his attention to Philip, smiling, straining toward him.

"I'm a newspaper reporter," he continued. "I was covering a story when I ran into your—into Harry down in Wales. This is pretty sensitive. I'm not sure how much I can tell you."

Jenny looked at him, resignation on her face. Nothing could surprise her anymore.

"Well, Mr. No-name reporter," she said, "you can tell me your real name at least, can't you?"

"It's Philip. I didn't mean to deceive you like that but, as I say, it's probably best you don't know all the details."

Little Harry stumbled over to Philip, who cuffed him gently, and pulled him onto the bed.

"It has to do with Harry," Jenny said, "and that top-secret stuff he mentioned in his letter, doesn't it?"

"Yes, I'm afraid so."

"Is that why he was dispatched on such short notice to North Africa?"

"I can only surmise."

She stared at him.

"Possibly, I can't be sure," Philip said. "But beyond that—"

"Yes?"

"His sudden disappearance," Philip said, his face edged with fear. "It's quite possible, I mean . . ."

"You think it could be foul play?"

Philip stared at her and nodded. He looked down at little Harry and rubbed his head gently.

"What about you, love?" Jenny said. "This story you're after puts you in the same fix, doesn't it?"

"I really haven't dwelled on it that much. But it could be possible."

She reached over and stroked his cheek. "Is it too late to . . ."

"To back out?" he said.

"Can you do that?"

"I—no," he said. His face was set. "No, I couldn't if I wanted to."

"Do you want to?" She searched his eyes for the truth.

"No," he said. "That's impossible. Call it what you will—

obstinateness, compulsion, a bloody disease. But I couldn't let go."

"I understand, I think," she said.

"I came here," Philip said, "because it was the only lead I had. I needed to talk to you. At first I thought that's all it was, following up a lead. Then . . ."

He looked directly into her eyes, touched her arm.

"Then you thought, why not have a bit of skirt while you're at it?"

"Jenny!"

"Just teasing." She snuggled against him and put her finger to his lips. "We don't have to put a label on it, love. Just let it be. I'm concerned about you—Philip. I wish you could let it go, but I know you can't."

"I wish I could too. It would simplify my life immeasurably. But . . ." He shrugged his shoulders.

"You needn't tell more than you can," she said. "But do be careful. I do care about you, you know?"

"I care about you too, Jenny," he said. "You and the little one here."

Philip put his arm around her and pulled her against his side. Little Harry gurgled and, for a moment, there was an illusion of peace in the world.

CHAPTER TWENTY-TWO

October 1941

THE PRIME MINISTER was all business tonight, and that was exactly the way John Simon liked it. No movies, no brandy, no cigars. Well, perhaps a cigar would be all right. Somehow they served to take the edge off his disposition when he was feeling out of sorts.

Churchill could not sit down, not for long. No sooner would he settle into his armchair—ordinarily his favorite position—than he would struggle back up to his feet and pace in circles around the room. Simon observed him from his straight-back wooden chair, his feet planted squarely on the floor, his hands resting on his knees. He could not recall the last time he had seen the prime minister look so agitated.

"It's difficult to understand," Churchill said, "how Hitler managed to botch it so. We gave him what he wanted; the rest seemed academic."

"In light of what's transpired on the front," Simon said, "his speech in Berlin was quite extraordinary."

"Sheer bombast," Churchill said. "Bombast and outright

lies. He's botched it badly and now he's trying to rewrite history while it's happening."

"Still, there have been some victories lately," Simon said.

"Victories, you say!" Churchill glared at him. The effect was disquieting. "What's difficult to understand is how few of them there are! He's put himself in a position where the slightest triumph is a cause for celebration. He had every conceivable advantage—well-fed troops, superior equipment, morale—and he's failed to capitalize on them. Even the weather was not a problem, though, Lord knows, it is now. Or will be soon."

Simon, also amazed, shook his head from side to side. "It *is* quite shocking," he said softly.

"It's more than shocking, John," Churchill said. "It's nothing short of mystifying. One can only hope that the Gerries don't get routed too quickly. A long, drawn-out campaign in the east was what we had hoped for."

"I've thought about little else for weeks now. But perhaps it'll work out yet the way we planned."

"Indeed." Churchill looked at him sharply. "All we asked for was a little time. A stalemate. Anything but a quick rout on either side. Let's hope that's not what we're faced with."

Simon did not think the situation on the eastern front was quite as bleak as the prime minister portrayed it, but there was no convincing him otherwise today. Besides, there were more immediate concerns right here at home. The Hess affair for one. As though reading his thoughts, Churchill said, "Hess seems to be truly going bonkers, if he wasn't before. Throwing fits, frightening the maid. What's the latest on him now?"

"We have him under constant watch. His flat is wired from front to rear, there's even a camera in the lighting fixture in his study. He seems to be writing some sort of manuscript."

Churchill paused in midstride and looked at Simon.

"Writing?" he said.

"A journal or some such thing. It's not clear."

"Well let's find out. I think that should be top priority, don't you?"

"Easier said than done. It's not as though he goes out and saunters about for any length of time. He's always close by, down in his garden, on the patio. He may even keep it with him—on his person, I mean."

The prime minister stood rooted in place, staring at John Simon.

"This is urgent business, John," he said. "I think we should find out what's in those notes. Good Lord! We can't allow him to compromise us in any way. Suppose he's keeping a diary of his mission to Scotland? Why wasn't I told of this before?"

"Just learned of it myself this morning. You're the first to know."

"The *only* one I should think! This has to remain absolutely confidential. Can we get someone in there to make a film? Perhaps he can be taken for a long stroll around the grounds."

"My thought precisely." There was a note of weariness in Simon's voice. Naturally, the job of taking Hess for a stroll would fall to him. He would have to face the man again.

"When's the last you saw him?"

"It's been some weeks," Simon said. "There've been so many pressing matters."

"None more urgent than this," Churchill said. "It's important to keep on him. I know it's not the most pleasant of assignments. Now, what about this chap Renfield?"

"We've got two of our best men monitoring his every move. At the moment, he's found a safe harbor for himself with the leftenant's widow."

"He shan't stay there for long, I don't think? He's got to move sooner or later."

"We'll know as soon as he does."

"What do you think he'll do next?" Churchill said.

"Difficult to say. Putting myself in his boots, I'd say it's only a question of time before he attempts to make contact with Hess himself."

"Indeed." The prime minister stopped and looked at Simon, then resumed his pacing around the room.

"Of course," Churchill said. "There's no other avenue left for him, is there? He's learned about as much as he possibly can from third parties. His only hope of tying up all the loose ends is to go up there himself, confront the man directly."

Simon studied the prime minister, who continued his circular pacing.

"I'll leave tomorrow morning," Simon said. "You're quite right. I have been neglecting our visitor lately. It's time I rectified the situation. I'll alert intelligence to slip a man in there with a camera as soon as I get Hess off alone."

Churchill stopped his pacing and looked directly at Simon. "Failing that, John . . . ," he said.

"Yes?"

"Perhaps we can use our reporter friend to retrieve the diary for us."

IN HIS JOURNAL, Hess wrote:

What had concerned the Führer more than anything was Stalin's reluctance to join him in the attack on Poland. Hitler believed, and rightly so, I think, that Stalin was biding his time until Germany made the first move. He was hoping to conserve the strength of his own forces until he had a better understanding of how well Hitler's plan was going to succeed.

Finally, after several visits to Moscow by Ribbentrop to voice the Führer's displeasure, Stalin decided to take action. At two o'clock on the morning of September 17, 1939, the Red Army crossed over into the Polish frontier. German intelligence units were able to ascertain that the conduct of the Russian troops was less than admirable. When the first advance forces encountered a crack contingent of the Polish Frontier Corps, they threw down their arms and shouted, "Don't shoot! We're here to help you against the Germans." It was only later, when the Red Army support forces came up from the rear waving white flags and the Poles were lured into complacency, that the Red Army opened fire and massacred them as they slept around their campsites.

After the fall of Poland, Ribbentrop was furious that Goebbels got all the credit for the victory when he informed foreign correspondents about it at a news conference in Berlin. He blamed Goebbels for trickery, but in reality Ribbentrop had himself to blame. His adjutant was unable to rouse him from his bed before eight o'clock on the morning following the victory, so stupefied was he from all the brandy he consumed the night before.

The friendship between the Führer and Stalin was doomed almost from the start. Stalin refused to lend his signature to a joint communiqué their aides drew up, and insisted on extensive revisions exaggerating his own role in the campaign. No sooner did the Führer accede to his wishes, for the sake of unity, than Stalin issued another demand. He would only agree to sign, he said, if Hitler agreed to an out-and-out partition of Poland that left the Poles without any semblance of independence. Actually, this was just as favorable to Germany as it was to the Russians, but the Führer distrusted Stalin's intentions to such a degree that it took him four days before he agreed to it.

Ribbentrop arrived in Moscow at 5:50 on the evening of September 27, to conclude the treaty with Stalin. He faced the treacherous Bolshevik leader with much trepidation, fearing that the price of a final agreement might be too high. Stalin began by offering Germany all Polish territory east of the Vistula, and in return he said he wanted only the third Baltic state, Lithuania, for himself. Since most of Poland's Jews lived in the territory Stalin was ceding to Germany, Stalin was in effect allowing Hitler to deal with them in any manner he saw fit.

Hitler felt that the loss of Lithuania was a heavy price to pay to appease the Russian leader, but he authorized Ribbentrop to sign the treaty anyway. In the back of his mind, the Führer was already formulating the details for Operation Barbarossa. It was just a question of time, he reasoned, before Germany invaded the east and seized everything he had given to Stalin by force from a weak, poorly equipped Red Army. Even so, his distrust of the two-faced Russian bear was total. If he didn't stop Stalin first, he knew that Stalin would turn against Germany the first instant he felt he could do so with impunity.

At this point in time, as far as Great Britain is concerned, the Führer has special plans for the British people after the war. Once he stood in awe of them, but now he is convinced that they can never be treated as equals. They are a decadent people, not to be trusted as coconspirators who deserve to share power with the Reich once the New Order is established.

The Führer has ignored the advice of his military advisers for too long. He permitted one opportunity after another to fade into history. Britain could have been taken with a minimum of effort, her cities bombed to extinction and her indolent people put to work in German mines and factories, their spines stiffened with a healthy dose of German discipline. Instead, by hesitating as he did, the Führer only succeeded in giving Churchill time to build up his forces.

Rudolf Hess laid down his pen, rubbed his eyes and reread the words he had written that morning. Satisfied that he had put down the facts and his thoughts as truthfully as possible, he closed his notebook and stuck it down inside his trousers, beneath his shirt, safe from nosy charwomen. Surely they had him under observation. He sensed the eyes and ears of his hosts monitoring his every move.

Hess turned on his radio. After listening impatiently to fifteen minutes of music, he finally heard news of the war. There were new German victories on the eastern front, the commentator said. The Germans had taken Bryansk, a major

Soviet stronghold south of Moscow, and General Guderian's panzer forces had succeeded in encircling three entire Red Army divisions. The fall of Moscow itself was now regarded as a distinct possibility by the Allies.

"Hah!" Hess jumped to his feet. "I knew it," he said out loud to the empty room. "Lies, propaganda I heard before. Now I am hearing the truth!"

Too bad Lord Chancellor Simon wasn't here now to share this moment with him. The man was so typical of his race—brilliant, clever and deceitful. A worthy adversary, but not to be trusted. You couldn't believe anything he said. He enjoyed sparring with Simon, matching wits with him and letting him know that Rudolf Hess was not a man to be trifled with. When the war was finally over—and won—the John Simons of the world would no longer be in a position to manipulate anyone.

CHAPTER TWENTY-THREE

JENNY, THE BOY, the squalid flat, the pot of Earl Gray brewing on the counter—all were becoming fixtures in his life. How comfortable it was. Too comfortable. There was a story to be uncovered, work to be done, and Philip was letting time slip by while he cuddled in his new nest.

Was it merely the warmth and comfort, or was it something else? Perhaps fear. What else could it be? There was no other name for it. Heart-chilling, shriveling fear. He had covered sensitive stories in the past, put himself at some risk. But never like this. The stakes were higher now than ever before.

Still, no one had forced him to come this far down the road. He had had ample opportunity along the way to give it up, play it safe, stay in Glasgow and interview old ladies for the social page. Perhaps Susan had been right. Why be a hero? Stick your neck out for no good end? What was the point? There had to be a good reason for what was going on. Some things were best left alone.

But that was not his way, had never been. He had chosen

this road willingly and was being compensated for his effort. Old man Buchanan was paying him to uncover a story, not to set up housekeeping in Liverpool. He looked across the table at Jenny, who sipped her tea and studied him over the rim of her cup. Little Harry breathed steadily as he napped in his crib. This would not be easy.

"I've got to go away for a few days," he said, "possibly a week or longer. Then I'll be back."

Jenny put down her cup and looked away. She did not speak.

"Soon as I've finished, I'll be back. Promise."

Jenny still did not reply.

"Nothing to say?" he asked.

"What's there to say?" she said. "The old story, isn't it? People come and go all the time, don't they?"

"It's not like that. I've got a job to do and I've been putting it off, but I can't any longer. I've got to . . ."

"You're going back where you met Harry, aren't you? You told me yourself you couldn't let it go, so I'm not surprised."

"You sound hurt all of a sudden. You knew I had to leave sooner or later."

"I was hoping it'd be later, that's all," she said. "You said yourself Harry wasn't sent away by chance."

Philip hesitated a moment.

"No, I don't suspect he was," he said.

"Whatever it is you're onto, whatever Harry told you, it's something that can only put you in harm's way. It certainly did him. He's gone, and now I'm about to lose you as well."

Philip squirmed uneasily in his chair, looked down at his untouched tea, started to light a cigarette, then thought better of it.

"I don't think it's the same for me," he said. "It isn't that easy. I mean, they can't just dispatch anybody they please."

"Good Christ, Philip. How can you be so—they can do any

bloody thing they want! You can disappear in an instant and who would care really, except for me?"

She reached out and touched his hand. Her eyes were moist, searching deep inside him.

"I *would* care, Philip," she said, "and that's all that matters to me. Can't you leave it alone, whatever it is?"

Philip took both her hands in his and looked into her eyes. "I care about you too, Jenny," he said. "And I also care what happens to me. I don't take foolish risks, not for nothing. But this is so big . . ."

"Not bigger than your life, I don't think. Oh, what's the use of talking? You'll do what you want anyway."

"What I *have* to do. We all have a job to do."

"Yours is not to get yourself killed."

"And I'm not going to. It won't take long—a week, two at the most. Then I'll be back. I promise you, Jenny."

She looked away, fighting back tears, then turned to him.

"Yes, I believe you will," she said. "If you can. I do believe that. Well, let's tidy up, shall we? His nibs'll be awake any moment, howling for his supper. You've barely touched your tea."

"I feel the need for something stronger," he said. "I could use a nip or two of whiskey. You?"

She looked at him sternly, then relaxed and broke into a laugh.

"You're an exasperating man, Philip Renfield. Drive any girl to drink. Pour a double for both of us then, love."

GOEBBELS SAT AT the table in the tiny room at the Wolf's Lair, notepad in front of him and pen at the ready. His nose twitched involuntarily; the air was moist and heavy. A medicinal pall permeated everything, and the room reeked of too much human proximity under less than ideal circumstances.

But the Führer seemed impervious to it all. His mood today was buoyant, almost jubilant. His high spirits would have been contagious had it not been for the dismal surroundings. Today, for the first time in weeks, there were genuine grounds for optimism. The tide was turning, and Hitler had special instructions for the hapless Goebbels on how to best handle the propaganda value of Germany's latest victories.

"Write this down exactly as I say," Hitler ordered as he paced back and forth in the narrow space, thinking as he strode, pausing each time his thoughts were organized. "This is absolutely urgent, Joseph, there must be no deviation."

Goebbels' misery was complete. He hid his clubfoot beneath his chair, out of Hitler's sight, transcribing the Führer's thoughts precisely as he spoke them.

"The Soviets are defeated, there is no question of that. That is exactly how the newspapers are to report it. Got that, Joseph? No ifs, whens, maybes, there's been too much of that already. You've allowed the press to publish too much negativity. Militarily, this war has already been decided. What remains to be done now is predominantly of a political nature—at home and abroad. At the same time—and this is critical—the German people cannot allow themselves to grow complacent because of our military victories. The people must harden themselves for many years of sacrifice. It is the task of the press—under your direction, Joseph—to help strengthen the resolve of the masses. When that is accomplished, the rest will follow of its own accord, so that"—Hitler stopped inches in front of his propaganda minister and stared directly into his eyes—"within a very short period, no one will notice that no peace has been concluded at all. Have you got all that down, Joseph?!"

"Yes, my Führer!"

Hitler's face was alight. The fire from his eyes hit Goebbels like a blast from a furnace. Goebbels started to speak but faltered. Panic gripped his entire body.

"So, Joseph. I want the word to go out through all media organs immediately!"

"Yes, Führer. It is brilliant, my Führer, absolutely . . ."

"You understand, Joseph?"

"Perfectly."

"You see how urgent it is to maintain morale? Never, for one instant, should the people be permitted to entertain thoughts of defeat. Never! At the same time, while they are learning of our magnificent victories in the east, they must be hardened to endure years—decades, if necessary—of continuing sacrifice. Because, Joseph, my struggle—our struggle—Germany's struggle—will not end with the fall of Russia. It will continue until the entire world is part of the Third Reich."

To Goebbels' relief, Hitler's attention was diverted from him by a knock on the door.

"Who is it?" Hitler shouted.

"It's Oberleutnant Heim, Führer. A dispatch from the front."

"Come in!"

The door opened and Heinrich Heim entered the cramped room, extending a dispatch toward the Führer.

"Read it!" Hitler's jaw was set, his eyes fixed on the far wall.

"It's from General Guderian, Führer. It states, 'Our tanks have reached the suburbs of Moscow, stop. Panic is sweeping the city, stop. Stampedes at all railroad stations leaving Moscow, stop. Communist Party officials fleeing by foot and car heading for Kuibyshev in the east, stop. Stalin said to be among them, stop.' "

Oberleutnant Heim finished reading and stood at attention,

waiting for instructions. Goebbels sat rigidly in his chair, staring up at Hitler. The Führer continued to look at the far wall for several moments until, finally, a stream of tears rolled down his cheeks and a tight-lipped smile of contentment crossed his face.

CHAPTER TWENTY-FOUR

Rᴜᴅᴏʟꜰ Hᴇss ɢʟᴏᴡᴇʀᴇᴅ at the elegant figure of John Simon, who entered the room, removed his gloves, and returned his stare.

"You have neglected me for many weeks," Hess said. "Can you deny it?"

"You're quite right," Simon said. "Unfortunately, it was unavoidable. If I could split myself in three, I'd find life easier all around. Have you been able to find enough to do? I'm sure this is all very tedious for you."

"I have my garden, my music, my sketch pad, my radio—everything but your challenging company."

Simon smiled. You have your journal too, he thought.

"Please accept my apologies," he said. "We have much to discuss. Shall we take a stroll around the grounds? It's a lovely day, perhaps one of the last of the season before the chill sets in."

Hess bowed slightly from the waist and clicked his heels.

"As you wish," he said.

The two men left the flat through the door that led to the garden. The day was slightly overcast, not nearly as delightful as Simon suggested, but Hess made no comment. They continued along a path that led past the rows of daffodils and tulips Hess had planted, then beyond the gazebo at the far end.

"You've quite a green thumb, I see," Simon said.

"Green . . . ?"

"Sorry. Quite a gift for gardening, I should say."

"Ah, yes. One of the great pleasures of life. Your prime minister, I understand, is also a man of the soil."

Simon laughed. The spectacle of Winston Churchill bending over in a garden, poking around in the soil, seemed irresistibly funny.

"Mr. Churchill enjoys the results of efforts such as yours," Simon said, "not the actual—um—exertion."

Would he ever understand the British, Hess wondered? Such a strange sense of humor. He never knew whether to laugh or shake his head in puzzlement.

Simon led the way along the footpath into the woods, and Hess followed slightly to the rear. This was the same path he used to take on his outings with the fat Leftenant Wilkins who disappeared so suddenly. He missed the outings, if not the company.

"It feels good to stretch out my boundaries again," Hess said. "My exercise has been confined to the garden since I last saw you."

"Yes. Your lack of personal lebensraum," said Simon, "is another one of those unfortunate inconveniences you've had to endure."

"From what I hear on the wireless," Hess said, "the fall of Moscow is only a matter of days. What news have you from the Führer?"

"Nothing more than you've apparently heard yourself."

"Nothing of my wife, my family?"

Simon stopped abruptly, and turned to face Hess.

"Your wife has been placed in detention by your beloved Führer." Simon did not attempt to hide the unfriendliness in his voice. "I know you don't want to believe that, but it's true. It is also true that your adjutant Karl Pintch has been arrested for conspiracy in the planning of your flight, and the Haushofers have been seized for failing to reveal their Jewish heritage. But I don't suppose anything I can say will convince you of that, or of the fact that you, yourself, would be in the utmost danger should you return to your homeland. Apparently, your friend the Führer has left you out on a limb."

The two men stood quite still, holding each other's gaze. Finally, Hess spoke. "Again, Sir John, I am willing to return and face the consequences. This is all for public appearance. The Führer cannot do otherwise. It is in accordance with the official position—yours and ours—on the incident."

"Perhaps in the beginning," Simon said, "but that's no longer true. Hitler will deal with you in the most expedient manner possible."

"Please?"

"In other words, dear fellow," Simon continued, "he can't take the risk of having you or anyone involved with you walking around freely. Silence—permanent silence, I daresay—is the only viable remedy."

"What you are suggesting, Lord Chancellor, is . . . unthinkable!" Rudolf Hess stood rigid with emotion, his honor offended. "I have been by the Führer's side for twenty years. My loyalty is unquestioned."

But your usefulness at this point may not be, thought Simon.

"This is just another example of your Jew—of your English treachery," Hess said.

Simon stared at his adversary, his lips tightening into a hard

smile. "Great Britain has honored every syllable of our agreement with your country! Regardless of the continuing dispu-
tation concerning that agreement, we have stood by it. I need
no lectures on treachery from you."

Once again, they regarded each other in silence. Again,
Hess spoke first.

"I demand that I be returned to the Fatherland without
further delay," he said. "There is no longer any excuse for my
detainment here. Your own radio reports say that the campaign in the east is all but won."

"The information we are receiving from the eastern front is
contradictory at best," Simon said. "Every day the momentum swings back and forth, the campaign hangs in the balance."

"Not so. The military conflict has already been decided in
Germany's favor. Only an official surrender remains, and the
political partition of the land and peoples."

"Astounding," Simon said.

"So?"

Simon studied the Deputy Führer of the Third Reich as
though attempting to divine the nature of his soul through his
eyes.

"I'm quite at a loss for words," Simon said. "You're beyond
logic."

"You deny my facts?"

"You'll believe what you want to believe, you're incapable
of doing otherwise."

"How do you respond?"

"Sir?"

"Your response, please. To my demand that I be permitted
to return to my homeland."

Simon looked at Hess, then shook his head slowly from side
to side.

"Permission denied." Simon turned suddenly in the other

direction and walked back toward the gazebo in the near distance. Hess stood his ground and called out after him, "Denied for what reason, Sir John?"

Simon did not pause to answer. He continued past the gazebo into the garden, leaving Rudolf Hess smoldering with indignation in the quiet forest.

TOM MOPPED THE bar with a soiled rag, then returned a moment later with two pints of half and half for the workmen at the end. He extracted a bent cigarette from a crumpled pack of Woodbines, and was about to light it when Philip Renfield entered the barroom from the hotel lobby. Tom exchanged a quick glance with one of the old workmen, then sauntered down the length of the bar to greet Philip as he helped himself to an empty stool.

"Well, you're a sight for sore eyes," Tom said. "Haven't seen you in—how long has it been now?"

"Three months or more, I'd say. At least that."

"What's your pleasure tonight, sir?"

"Whiskey, I think," Philip said. "A double, with a dash of soda water."

"Taking a bit of holiday again, are you?" Tom asked when he returned with Philip's drink.

"Yes. The wife and I've put an end to it once and for all. Felt a need to get off on my own a bit, you know how it is."

"Indeed I do. Been through it myself a time or two, I'm sorry to say. It's never easy."

"Don't suppose it is," Philip said.

"Did you ever meet up with your leftenant friend," Tom said, "the one you had drinks with that evening?"

"No. Why, hasn't he been back since?"

"Not a sign of him. Popped in regularly for the longest time, then disappeared without so much as a fare-thee-well.

It *is* wartime and all that. I reckon National Service had better use for him fighting wogs someplace."

"Sounds that way."

"And how long will you be staying with us this time, if you don't mind my asking?"

"Not at all. Shouldn't be more than three days, four at most. Long enough to clear my head and get on with things."

"If we can make your stay more comfortable in any way," Tom said, "don't hesitate to ask."

Tom moved down the bar to take care of two customers whose glasses needed refilling. Cigarette and pipe smoke hung heavily in the air. Dampness clung to everything; it was palpable, and carried with it a chill that seeped right through to the bone. From the corners of his eyes, Tom could see Philip lighting up a cigarette, then covering his mouth as a convulsive cough raked his body. After several minutes, drinks poured and his other customers content for the moment, Tom moved back along the bar toward Philip.

"Nasty cough there," Tom said. "Terrible time of year what with all the cold and damp setting in."

"Don't have much choice, do we?" Philip said. "It's a national affliction. Can't very well go off to sunny climes with the war on and all."

"Not bloody likely. Doesn't seem as though it's likely to end anytime soon, does it, the way it's going. Would you like another?"

"One more, I think, then I'll be off. Want to tuck in early and get an early start, take some exercise in the morning, take a look at the abbey and such."

Tom poured Philip's drink and mopped the bar.

"Quite a sight, those ruins," he said. "Pity you didn't have time to see them on your last visit."

"I'd other things on my mind then," Philip said, "than taking in the sights. Wondering whether to patch things up with the wife and all. Some time off on my own now'll do me good."

"Can't say I envy you," Tom said, "going through a thing like that. Sooner or later it hits us all—separation, I mean, one kind or another."

"True enough. Doesn't make it easier, though." Philip raised his glass and finished off half his drink in one swallow. Tom rapped the bar with his knuckles, a good-luck gesture, then walked down to the other end.

EARLY THE FOLLOWING morning, Philip ate a hearty breakfast of porridge, kippers and a single egg with toast and jam, then left the Angel Hotel for his walk in the hills. He was wearing a brown woolen cap, a khaki commando-style sweater beneath a brown duffel outercoat, coarse bird-watching trousers and leather lace-up boots with heavy soles. He carried a stout walking stick in his right hand, binoculars around his neck and a light canvas pack on his back.

Tom the bartender watched him leave, then walked over to the telephone behind the front desk. He picked up the receiver and dialed a number.

"He's just left," he said to the man on the other end. "Should be passing by your post within the hour. No, no, listen up. Our orders are to let him pass. Got that now? Don't ask me, I only do what I'm told myself. That's it now. Let him pass. Spread the word."

CHAPTER TWENTY-FIVE

OBERLEUTNANT HEIM STOOD at attention in the stifling room as the Führer raged at him from three feet away. There was nothing to say, nothing to do but stand and take it until his fury was spent. It had nothing to do with him personally, Heim knew. Everyone had told him, don't be the one to deliver bad news to Hitler, delegate that job to an underling, anyone but yourself. But this time it was unavoidable. Hitler was aware that a dispatch had just arrived from the eastern front and ordered Heim to bring it to him at once.

"How can it be?" Hitler slapped the dispatch with the back of his free hand. "We had the city surrounded! People fleeing, soldiers panicking, Stalin running off like a dog with his tail between his legs!"

Heim stood rigidly, trying not to look at Hitler as he read the dispatch for the second time:

Stalin has rallied his forces, stop. Declared a state of siege, stop. Has ordered retreating soldiers shot without trial, stop.

Soviet reinforcements sent in from the east, stop. Panzer advance has slowed forty kilometers south of Moscow, stop. Weather turned abruptly worse with heavy rain and sleet, stop. Mark IVs mired down in mud, stop. Soviet T-34s lighter and more mobile in mud and snow, stop. Luftwaffe grounded due to low visibility, stop. Conditions now impossible for further advance, stop. Request permission to pull back twenty kilometers and regroup until weather breaks, stop. Guderian

"Traitor!" Hitler screamed. "Why do they sabotage me at every turn?"

Heim, not knowing whether to reply, remained silent.

"Why are they all against me?" Hitler's eyes bored holes right through his aide. "Victory is ours! Courage! Determination! There can be no retreat! Cowards do not win wars!"

Heim dared not move.

"Sit at the table and take this down. Quickly!"

"Yes, my Führer."

"Here is my answer: 'Permission denied, stop. Retreat is out of the question, stop. Hold your ground at all costs, stop. Reinforcements are on the way, stop. Luftwaffe will strike Moscow within hours as weather improves, stop. Resume your advance as soon as air support commences, stop. Adolf Hitler.' There, that ought to show him what I think of his request. Send it off. Now!"

Heim did not need any further encouragement to leave. But when a new dispatch came in from the front four hours later, this one signed by Field Marshal von Rundstedt, Heim's entire neurological apparatus was on the point of collapse. He approached Hitler's lair and knocked softly.

"What is it?"

"A new dispatch, Führer."

"Bring it to me."

Heim entered, extended the dispatch toward the Führer.

"Read it," Hitler said.

His voice quavering, Heim read, "We cannot attempt to hold, stop. If they do not retreat our troops will be decimated, stop. I request that this order be rescinded or you accept my resignation as commandant, stop. Field Marshal von Rundstedt."

To Heim's surprise, Hitler did not scream this time. In fact, he did not speak for a full two minutes, but merely stared at the far wall and smiled crookedly. Then, in the gentlest voice Heim had ever heard him use, Hitler said, "Take this down. 'I am acceding to your request, stop. You are replaced by Field Marshal von Reichenau effective immediately, stop. Adolf Hitler.' "

THE FIRELIGHT DID its eerie dance. It was the only illumination in the room. Blackness coated the windows beyond the drawn curtains, enveloping all of London. Blackout. The firelight jumped and danced in the fireplace in Churchill's study, casting leaping specters over the walls and ceiling and across the prime minister's face.

"Do you think that was wise, John, leaving him in the woods?" Churchill said.

He knew it was, they had been over it before, but Simon hid his irritation.

"I'm sure it was the best tack, the only one," Simon said.

"Perhaps. Couldn't find it anywhere, you say?"

"Not a sign of it on the premises."

"Hmmm." Churchill pondered a moment. Smoke rising from his Dunhill further obscured his visage. "Odd, isn't it?"

"There's only one plausible explanation," Simon said. "He keeps it on his person."

"So you stalked off and left him there, howling in the woods?"

Simon could feel the color in his cheeks, but he managed again to keep his voice even.

"I wanted to leave him with the understanding that he has nowhere else to turn. Employing Renfield as his agent of communication with the outside world is the only course left to him."

The prime minister laughed in that childish manner of his, the same way he laughed whenever he watched one of his beloved Marx brothers films.

"Lord, John, I'd love to have been there to see that. Love to have captured it on film."

John Simon did not think it was funny. He had been terrified out there with that lunatic, the sentries no closer than 200 meters away. Hess was big and strong—and younger. He might have pounced on Simon from behind, for all Simon knew. What did he have to lose? His freedom? Hess had already forsaken that. He could hardly be worse off than he was now. The very thought of it chilled Simon.

"Well, you're done with him now at least." Churchill was still smiling, puffing absently on his cigar, staring into the darting flames. "It's up to the reporter now."

"The sentries have been alerted to let him pass," Simon said. "Beyond that, it's out of our hands."

The prime minister turned away from the fire and faced Simon. There was no mirth in his eyes now, no smile on his lips. "I don't have to tell you, John, how critical a role you've played in this," he said. "The way you've dealt with Hess, your management of the entire affair has been exemplary."

John Simon nodded his head in thanks, but Churchill's statement set alarm bells ringing within. As always, there was a double edge to the prime minister's words, even his apparent compliments.

CHAPTER TWENTY-SIX

A HIGH, DENSE MIST enveloped the peaks of the Brecon Hills outside Abergavenny. The mist sat immutable and motionless. Later in the morning, the sun would rise above the ridge of the Black Mountains in the distance and the mist would break apart slowly in its timeless way. A dazzle of slanting yellow rays would stream down on the gray hills. Then the morning would be gone, and with it the timeless mist, and the hills would come alive with lush and sensuous green as the sun lowered toward the west on the far side of the mountains.

All that would come later. At this hour of the morning, the mist and the gray were everywhere. The air was cold and more than damp. It was beaded through with tiny droplets of water that coated Philip Renfield's face as he kept to the woods beside the path that ascended into the mountains. He could feel the wetness on his cheeks, and the raw cold air that tinted them with red. He made an effort to muffle the rumbling in his chest before it erupted to the surface in a spasm of coughing.

He moved deeper into the woods as he approached the first sentry post 300 meters up the hill. The forest was thick with oaks and maples, heavy undergrowth that rose up to form a thicket of prickly bramble, dense raspberry and blackberry bushes and other wild shrubbery. Tendrils snaked down from the trees, further impeding Philip's progress as he felt his way as quietly as possible through the verdant tangle. The air was fresh, a mingle of damp earth and green smells, and brought back memories of childhood days in the hills of Scotland. When this was over, he was going to go back there again.

It was slow going, slower than he had anticipated. Besides the heavy growth, the ground was uneven and he had to watch his footing. By his watch, it took him the better part of an hour to skirt the first sentry post and climb sufficiently far above it to feel he was out of danger. There was one more on the road ahead before he reached the final checkpoint leading into the hospital compound. How he would bypass that, and locate Hess once he was inside, was something he would determine later. Leftenant Wilkins had told him that the Nazi had been given a flat of his own, with a garden nearby where he puttered during the day.

It was late morning by the time he reached the point at which the woods began to thin out. Philip could now see the old Victorian mansion and the red brick buildings through the clearing. There was a guard post on the main road leading into the grounds. He stayed back where the trees were thick and provided him with good cover. After a while, he moved to his left and started to circle clockwise around the compound to learn the layout and get a feel for what was going on inside.

There was a fence partway around, Philip saw, but to his surprise the security seemed fairly lax. It would be easy for someone to wander off the grounds unobserved. Then again, why shouldn't it be? This was a hospital, not a prison. Hess would be closely watched, and he couldn't get very far on his own if he did decide to take a stroll. Philip's biggest concern was that there might be patrols out in the forest, and that they would see him before he spotted them.

Toward one o'clock he felt famished. It had been a hard morning's work, and it had put a sharp edge on his appetite. He found a coppice of trees surrounded by heavy brush, and decided to pause there for lunch. He had brought cheese and sausage from the hotel, tomatoes and good hard bread and a jar of water, enough to last him two meals and maybe a third if he had to stretch it that far. He pulled the backpack off, made a place on the ground, then sat down to eat. He forced himself to chew slowly, making it last and letting the fullness build inside. When he finished, he resisted the urge to light a cigarette. A fit of coughing out there in the quiet woods might undo him. After he finished, he rolled up the dirty paper and scraps of food and put them back inside the pack, leaving no trace behind.

An hour later, he found what he was looking for. A third of the way around the compound, behind the old mansion, was the entrance to a garden. He could see a gazebo just inside, on the far end closest to him. Philip's elation quickly turned to trepidation. Now that he had apparently reached his destination, what was he going to do?

Watch. And wait. But for what? For Hess to come outside? Then what? Walk up and say, Hello, how d'ya do? I'm Philip Renfield from the *Daily Record.* You must be Rudolf Hess, Deputy Führer of the Third Reich.

Philip chuckled, feeling absurd. What a fool. He had no plan. How could he have a plan? How did you plan for a meeting like this? All he could do was watch and wait. Then make his move, go on instinct, see what developed. Let his sixth sense as a reporter guide him from one moment to the next.

By six o'clock, neither Rudolf Hess nor anyone else had shown his face in the garden. The sun was setting in the west and the chill of evening began to work its way into Philip's bones. He began to wonder if perhaps he might be losing his mind. His predicament was quite bizarre. The mission that seemed so rational in the light of day now struck him as futile.

Leave it alone. Turn back, go down the hill, pretend you were gallivanting around the ruins all day. No one would be the wiser. Pack your bags in the morning and go back to Glasgow. Write stories about the Home Guard and the La- dies' Guild and forget all this.

But he had come so far, gone right out to the edge. If only . . .

If only he could get one glimpse of Hess and convince himself that the man wasn't mad after all. Hess was scarcely 200 meters away. Having come all this way, Philip couldn't return empty-handed, nagging doubts tormenting him the rest of his life.

One look, that's all. Just to be sure. Perhaps a word or two.

Of course he couldn't go back now. How could he even entertain the notion? *Of course* he had to follow through, complete the job he set out to do.

Philip set up camp again in the cover of the woods, the gazebo and the garden clearly in sight. The evening grew darker and colder, and he felt a need for food. He ate some more of the sausage and a small piece of bread, and washed it down with a swallow or two of water. Then, as total darkness settled in around him, blacking out the outlines of the trees and undergrowth, the buildings came alive with lights, one here, two there, suddenly a blaze of them illuminating the night. A light went on in the flat on the other side of the garden, and Philip's spirits started to soar once again.

Hess was inside. Enjoying his evening meal, perhaps, or settling in for an evening of reading.

Philip rolled up his food and put it back inside the pack. It was time to get going. He moved out of the blackness, closer to the edge of the light that reached out into the garden. Every sound was magnified a hundred times this time of day, every twig crunched underfoot, the brush of foliage against his clothing, the natural clatter of creatures raising their voices in nightsong.

He was inside the garden, just past the gazebo, keeping to the perimeter just beyond the circle of light. There was no backing away now, no going down the mountain without finishing what he had set out to do that morning—a million years ago.

Philip moved along the edge of the garden toward the flat. He quickened his pace. The light from within grew brighter. He was there, really there, in front of the door. He did not hesitate, could not hesitate.

He knocked three times softly, then stood back and listened to the night sounds in the distance.

CHAPTER TWENTY-SEVEN

VON RUNDSTEDT'S FACE was totally without expression as he stared at the Führer. His cold, dead eyes concealed the contempt and utter rage that churned away behind the passive mask. He had been packing to go home after being relieved of his command, when Hitler summoned him to the Wolf's Lair. The Führer tried to stare him down at close range, as he had done successfully with all the others, but von Rundstedt refused to be cowed. He held his ground, saying nothing, and waited for Hitler to speak his mind.

"In the future," Hitler said, "I will not tolerate any more resignations from my field marshals."

"I did not resign, Führer, I was relieved."

"It's all the same. I myself, for example, am not in a position to go to my superior, God Almighty, and say, 'I am not going on with it, I no longer want the responsibility.' "

Von Rundstedt's face revealed nothing—pity, alarm, contempt. "Responsibility is not the issue," he said. "I welcome responsibility. It is the conduct of the campaign I take issue with."

"I am Supreme Commander and your role is to follow my orders."

"Permit me, Führer, but a field marshal is not a mere"—he was about to say "mere corporal," then checked himself—"a mere puppet to be manipulated on strings. He has responsibility for his men, for lives, for the success or failure of his battle plan."

"I assume full responsibility," Hitler said. "Their lives, their souls, the weight of all Germany, the glory of the Reich is on my shoulders."

"Every officer in the field, everyone with firsthand information about the impossible conditions we are dealing with agrees with my assessment," said von Rundstedt. "It is suicide not to pull back under the circumstances."

Hitler stared at him, but did not reply immediately. Von Rundstedt knew he was on solid ground, knew that Hitler had received the same report not only from that lackey Paulus, but also from his old comrade Sepp Dietrich, commander of the SS Leibstandarte, whom he trusted as much as he could be said to trust anyone.

"Field Marshal von Reichenau will do precisely as I have instructed him." Hitler was implacable, as unyielding as von Rundstedt. "He will hold the ground we have won and finish the advance into Moscow."

"I wish that were so, Führer, but I fear it is not to be. You haven't heard the latest. Rostov has fallen to the Red Army."

Von Rundstedt's words cut deeply. He could see the pain in Hitler's face as he delivered the news that was only now unfolding in the east.

"Even as we speak, a greater disaster is looming on the central front. Not only is the offensive against Moscow foundering, but General Zhukov is already beginning a massive counteroffensive of one hundred divisions along a two-hundred-mile front. His troops have air and tank support while our men are still without overcoats and woolen stockings. The nights are bitter, the men are freezing, they have to light fires under the tanks to start the engines, the telescopic sights are useless, not designed for such cold. We waited far, far too long to launch our attack on Moscow, wasted too much time on Kiev, in the south . . ."

"Enough!" Hitler was trembling, his entire body quaking with rage. "These are lies, all lies!"

"Not lies, Führer—facts, reality. This is the truth."

"My other commanders are not as spineless as you!"

"Ask them, Führer. Field Marshal von Bock is shivering with fever and cramps, sick and discouraged. And Commander-in-Chief von Brauchitsch—"

"Von Brauchitsch is loyal and fearless. He will stick with me to the end."

"Ask him, Führer. As we speak, von Brauchitsch is already drawing up his papers. He is preparing to resign!"

RUDOLF HESS BENT over his journal, writing intently.

I took my place beside the Führer at the conference in the woods near Compiègne after France surrendered. Also seated at the long table that had been set up in an old railroad car for the occasion were Göring, Raeder, Brauchitsch and Ribbentrop. After we were all seated, the French delegation arrived, led by members of their armed forces and their former ambassador to Germany.

Hitler stood up, bowed slightly, and then everyone took their seats. Field Marshal Wilhelm Keitel read the armistice terms that had been dictated by Hitler, with my assistance and a little help from Ribbentrop. The terms were a masterpiece of strategic design, offering lenient terms to the French while at the same time attacking the English in the hope that they would accept the same honorable terms for themselves. The wording of the armistice, as best as memory serves me, was as follows:

"The aim of Germany's demands is to prevent a resumption of hostilities, to give Germany security for the further conduct of the war against England, which she has no choice but to continue, and also to create the conditions for a new peace that will repair the injustice inflicted by force on the German Reich."

As I previously stated, this was directed more at England than at France, which, after all, had no other choice but to accept any terms the Führer dictated. The hope was that England would agree to let Germany turn eastward in her drive for lebensraum in return for safe passage in the open seas. Most of Hitler's close advisers, including myself, supported the Führer in this strategy with the exception of . . .

Rudolf Hess's concentration was interrupted by what sounded like three soft knocks on the door. Could it be the wind, a branch blowing against the side of the building? No one visited him this time of night; no one visited him at all anymore.

"Yes?" he said.

No answer. Hess was about to turn back to his journal when again he heard three light raps on the door. Quickly, he folded up his notebook and tucked it down inside his shirt. He stood up, walked over to the door and put his ear against it.

"Is someone there?" he said.

"Can you let me in?" a voice said. "I'd like to speak to you, it's rather urgent."

"Who is there?"

"Please, open the door."

Hess paused a moment, then undid the latch. A thin, bedraggled man stood shivering on the doorstep. A cold breeze blew in and Hess felt the chill.

"Who are you?" he said.

"Thanks so much," the visitor said and entered the flat. "Do you speak English? You seem to understand. I'm taking on a lot being here, you know."

Hess closed the door and stared at the pale man with sandy hair and flushed cheeks. He looked rumpled, as though he had been wandering about for hours.

"Yes, I speak English," Hess said. The man stared back at him with relentless eyes, studying him from head to toe. "I am not accustomed to receiving visitors at such hours. You have taken me by surprise."

"Yes, well, sorry about that."

"Who are you?"

"Who I am is not important. Why I'm here is what counts. It's . . . it's absolutely critical."

"Yes?"

The young man looked around uneasily, unsure of himself. "We are alone, I take it?" he said.

"Alone? Yes, we are alone, all alone."

"Good. I mean, if anyone knew I had come here, you must understand—"

"You have been sent by someone?"

"Sent? Yes, I was sent," the visitor said.

"By whom? You have news for me?"

The man hesitated, looked around. He motioned toward the sofa in the living room.

"Do you mind?" he said. "I've been on my feet all day."

"Not at all." Hess waved him toward the sofa. "Some tea, perhaps, or . . ."

"Tea would be fine."

"I have brandy, if you would like."

The visitor paused a second, then replied, "Thanks, no. Tea will do."

Hess busied himself in silence for several minutes while the young man took off his damp outercoat and let the warmth of the flat penetrate inside him. He entered the living room carrying a tray with tea brewing in a pot, two cups and an assortment of biscuits.

"Here, let me help you with that," the man said.

"It's quite all right. Sit down, make yourself warm and comfortable and tell me who sent you here."

The visitor kept staring at him, studying him. Hess looked back and saw that his guest was not as young as he had at first appeared.

"What have they been telling you?" the visitor asked.

"Telling me?" repeated Hess. "They tell me nothing I can't hear on the wireless myself."

"Who's they, your liaison with London?" said the young man.

"John Simon. Is it he who sent you here? You must know him."

"Of course." The visitor sipped his tea, nibbling absent-mindedly on a biscuit as he stared into space. Hess was growing a trifle annoyed; he was none the wiser since the man arrived.

"Please, sir, your name," Hess said. "And your reason for coming here tonight."

"Ian MacDonald. I'm from Glasgow, Scotland, and I'm one of the men who were expecting you that night."

The man looked directly into Hess's eyes. Hess looked back. Glasgow. Expecting him. His spirits brightened just a bit.

"You have been sent by the duke then?"

"Hamilton, yes. I take it you haven't heard from him since—"

"Not a word. Only from Simon. You have news for me from the duke?"

"He's asked me to reestablish contact with you. What has Sir John been telling you?"

"Lies, only lies!" Hess stood up and started pacing across the room, back and forth. "My life is in danger if I return to Germany, he says. My wife is under house arrest, my adjutant, the Haushofers—all are in custody. He says the campaign in the east is going badly for the Reich, and even the propaganda on the wireless repeats his lies. I am imprisoned here against my will. I wish only to return to the front, to be with the Führer, where I belong, now that my mission is completed. Can you arrange this for me?"

"Yes," the visitor said. "But it won't be easy. Our contacts in Germany are waiting for some communication from you. They are concerned about you, they wonder how you are, how you are being treated. We in Scotland—the duke, the underground movement that arranged your mission—want to publicize your plight so the people can know the truth."

"Yes, yes. You can get word to the Führer? You can do all these things?"

"We can, but we need your cooperation. This is wartime and the government has put restrictions on the press. But there are other ways—the foreign press, our underground network. We want to make your story known and arrange for your return home. Can you help us in this?"

"Mr. Mac . . ."

"Call me Ian."

"Ian, I am only too happy to do whatever is necessary to accomplish this. Where can we start?"

"First, the duke would like a word from you. He's been isolated since you arrived. He needs to know exactly what Simon's been telling you."

"Only what I told you already," Hess said. "The duke is not on good terms with his superiors?"

"Everybody's afraid word will get out. You understand, it's very sensitive. He's been kept in the dark by London since you last saw him."

"He is in custody?" Hess said.

"Not exactly. Just under observation all the time. That's why I'm here. He sent me to let you know we're still behind you, still working quietly, as effectively as we can."

Hess sat down again and looked into the visitor's eyes. He hadn't felt this elated in months. There was hope. Germany's friends in England had not deserted him after all.

"We must be careful here too," Hess said in a whisper. He motioned around the room. "Perhaps even now we are being heard."

He saw the flicker of panic in the visitor's eyes. The pale man looked from left to right.

"You think . . . ," he started to say.

Hess silenced him by putting his finger to his lips. He stood up and motioned for the visitor to follow him. Hess opened the door quietly and stepped out into the garden. The young man followed and closed the door behind him.

"I should have thought of that myself," the man said.

"I have no proof, but one can't be too careful," Hess said.

"You're probably right, it makes sense."

Hess squared his shoulders and faced his guest directly. He was ten or twelve years older than the pale man, but three inches taller and twenty pounds of solid muscle heavier.

"Ian," Hess said.

"Yes?"

"The story you have told me is very encouraging. Before we proceed, however, I must protect myself. You must have some proof of who you are, that you were sent here by the duke."

The visitor hesitated. Something flashed through his eyes. Fear? Surprise? It was difficult to tell in the dark. Hess waited, watching, and stood his ground on the balls of his feet.

"Yes, I have proof," the pale man said.

Hess waited but did not speak.

"Of course you have to be careful," the man said. "I was with the duke that day. You did not see me, but I was there in the background. You remember the day they took that man out of Maryhill Barracks, the double they put in the Tower of London? You came out almost forty minutes later and were taken to a safe house in Pollockshields."

Hess relaxed, smiled, and sighed audibly.

"I was with the duke when he arranged it," the man said. "He told me to tell you that story if you asked."

Hess leaned forward and grasped the visitor warmly with both hands. He wanted to believe him, but how far could he trust him? It was important to be careful here, to separate what he wanted to hear from the facts.

"So it is true then." There were tears in Hess's eyes. It might pay to make the man think he had won Hess's confidence completely. "Finally, just when I thought all hope was lost."

"The duke sends his warmest regards. He hopes you are being treated well and wants you to know we haven't forgotten you, that we're doing everything we can to arrange safe passage for you back to Germany."

"I am comfortable, yes. I have enough food, my garden, the radio, music to listen to, only . . ."

"Yes?"

"It is the isolation. My only contact is with the lord chancellor and his lies. The news on the radio? It is propaganda, yes? The blitzkrig on the eastern front is going badly for the Reich? All this is true?"

"It's not as bad as it sounds," the visitor said. "There are difficulties. Problems with the weather have slowed things up a bit, and it appears there won't be an early victory, but it's not as dismal as the wireless would have one believe."

"And Churchill has honored his side of the agreement?" Hess said.

"Yes, of course," the visitor said, after hesitating for a second. "There's no question of that. None whatsoever. But the Russians have proved to be a bit more resilient than one might have imagined. It's taking longer than anticipated, but I don't think there's any question of the final outcome."

"Thank God!" Hess's eyes glistened in the dark. The pale man looked at him intently, his face almost luminous in the moonlight. If only he could be sure his visitor was who he said he was.

"Whatever John Simon's been telling you," the man said, "is tailored to suit his own interests. But we—the duke, myself, others who work with us—are trying to get the truth to the British people. There's no question in my mind that the public will see things our way once the facts are known."

"Yes, yes, the Führer has felt all along that Germany and England have a common destiny. It is only political forces in your country that keep it from being realized. We are allies against the decadence of the barbarians."

"I couldn't agree with you more," the visitor said. "If only there were some way of getting this message out to the public, the world, our friends in America."

"America too. Precisely!" Hess looked at the man, who appeared young once again with the moonlight glowing in his face. Was it destiny that brought him here tonight? Should he trust him with—there was so little time. He had to make a decision immediately. It was only a question of time before the British searched his room—searched him *bodily* perhaps—and discovered his journal. It would be safer in the hands of friends, if he was a friend. The moment of decision was at hand.

"I have something for you. A document."

"A document?"

"Yes, a history I have been making of the Führer's sacred mission, of the Reich, of the glorious philosophy that has driven Germany to fulfill her divine destiny. It tells of the inspiration for *Mein Kampf*—which I helped the Führer create—the history behind it and also what will follow when the war is finally won."

Hess reached inside his shirt and the pale man's eyes widened. The Deputy Führer of the Third Reich pulled out a worn notebook, which he held in both hands as though he were handling a sacred scroll.

"I have decided to entrust this to you," Hess said. "To you and the duke. It is for the world to see. Once the civilized peoples in England and America read my document, there will be a great uprising against all those who oppose the Führer and the Reich, against everyone who defiles the glory of the Fatherland."

The visitor accepted the notebook and tucked it quickly inside his own shirt.

"You've done a wonderful thing," he said. "I'll do everything in my power to see that your document is widely published. You have my sacred vow on that."

"You will visit me again?" Hess said.

"In a few days, a week at the most. Just as soon as I speak to the duke and the others in the movement."

"I will have more for you then."

"And I'll have more news for you as well."

Rudolf Hess straightened his back, brought his heels together, and thrust his right arm out in front of him.

"Heil Hitler!" he said.

The visitor's arm rose slowly in the air and he came to attention. He looked directly into Hess's eyes and said in a firm voice, "Heil Hitler!"

CHAPTER TWENTY-EIGHT

November 1941

ON OCTOBER 31, a German submarine fired a torpedo at the U.S. destroyer *Reuben James*, which had been escorting a convoy of merchant ships 600 miles west of Iceland. Hitler had instructed his U-boat commander, Grand Admiral Erich Raeder, to avoid any unnecessary "incidents" with American merchant ships unless he was convinced they had entered Icelandic waters with materiel bound for Russia. The torpedo found its mark, and the *Reuben James* sunk out of sight in the icy northern waters with 101 American sailors aboard.

Overnight, isolationist sentiment in the United States was dealt a fatal blow—five weeks before the bombing of Pearl Harbor. On November 7, a month before Japanese bombs rained down on the American naval base in Hawaii, Adolf Hitler climbed aboard his private railroad car at the Wolf's Lair and embarked on a journey to Munich, the place he regarded as his spiritual home, the city where his National Socialist Party had established its foundation.

The hall was packed with party loyalists, Nazi tricolor banners covered the walls and radio microphones embellished with eagles and swastikas encircled the podium. For the occasion, Hitler had worn his long rubberized gray field coat and gray cap with shining black peak that appeared to be a size too large for his head. It rested on the tops of his ears, and the peak obscured the top half of his face.

"President Roosevelt," he screamed into the microphones, "has finally succumbed to the Jewish cabal in America. He has ended all pretense of neutrality, and entered our waters with critical supplies for our mortal enemy to the east. I have ordered any German officer court-martialed who fails to defend himself against these unprovoked attacks.

"We will outlast this President Roosevelt, I swear it. We can afford to wait and take our time to win this war in our own way. This is the Reich and it will last for a thousand years to come."

Hitler paused, measuring his cheering audience, and slapped a glove into his left palm.

"No power on earth can shake the German Reich now," he continued. "Divine Providence has willed it that I fulfill our great Germanic mission. Churchill and Roosevelt are sitting over there in their plutocratic little world, surrounded and enslaved by everything that's become obsolete in the last decade. The moneybags run the show behind the scenes, while a parliamentary circus tramples on what is left of the rights and privileges of the people. I have my people behind me, and they have faith in me, their Führer."

Hitler stopped again and let the screams of his audience run their course. He continued, "I have plans to work for my people for the next fifty years. I don't need a war to stay in office like the Daladiers and Chamberlains and Churchills. And, for that matter, Herr Roosevelt of America. Yes, Herr Roosevelt and his Jews. He wants to run the world and rob us all of our place in the sun. He says he wants to save England, but he really means he wants to be the heir and ruler of the British Empire.

"Roosevelt is a fanatic!" Hitler screamed. Anyone close enough to study his eyes would have detected the fear in them. "I will crush him. There is absolutely no possibility of Germany remaining at peace with the United States while he is in power. I am determined on this point. War with America is inevitable!"

SIR JOHN SIMON was not at his best without a good night's sleep, and he had not slept well for three nights in a row. Dark circles rimmed his eyes, his cheeks were doughy and pale, his body sagged, and he suddenly looked like a man on the threshold of old age.

"Disappeared, you say?" Churchill removed the Dunhill from his mouth and stared at Simon. Adversity, it seemed, only served to make him feistier. "For more than eight hours? That's extraordinary, John, positively extraordinary. Let's take it through step-by-step one more time, shall we?"

John Simon did not want to take it through one more time. They had been through it enough times already, but the prime minister was quite insistent.

"We know he left the hotel in early morning," Simon said. "Our man there watched him leave with scarcely enough food to last him twenty-four hours."

"How was he dressed?" asked the prime minister.

"For the occasion." Simon heaved a sigh. "Duffel coat, proper walking boots, woolen cap and sweater, a satchel for his supplies. It was as though, as he had told the barman, he was off for a day's outing in the hills."

Churchill paced across the room, puffing absentmindedly on his cigar, his eyes on the carpet as though searching there for answers.

"And he arrived at the hospital grounds when?" he said.

"Late morning," said Simon. "Passed the first checkpoint within the hour, the second an hour after that. He was spotted in the woods outside the compound shortly before noon."

"And then?"

"Our information is sketchy after that. He began circling around the grounds in a clockwise fashion, keeping to the woods, then—unfortunately—we lost him," Simon said.

"How so, John?" Churchill stopped his pacing, turned about and stared at Simon. Simon had anticipated the question—it was their third run-through of the performance—and he looked back at the prime minister.

"Our men thought it best not to run the risk of frightening him off. They knew his destination, knew they'd pick him up again once he made contact with Hess."

"Which he did?"

"Yes, at precisely eight forty-seven in the evening."

"So we know nothing of his whereabouts or activity," Churchill said, "from noon till eight forty-seven, a period of nearly nine hours in duration."

"Presumably he was hiding out in the woods. Not much else for him to do out there but bide his time."

Despite his attempt at self-control, John Simon failed to keep the sarcasm completely out of his voice. The prime minister enjoyed making people state the obvious when there was no apparent reason for it.

"I disagree, John," Churchill said. "He might've been spotted by someone else in that time, perhaps even spoken to someone."

"Not likely. At any rate, there was no alternative, for the reason I already gave. Our men were determined not to frighten him off before he completed his mission. His activities in the forest were of little consequence compared to the outcome of his encounter with Hess."

Churchill stared at Simon, saying nothing. Simon had difficulty shaking off his vague feeling of inadequacy.

"Our main concern," Simon continued, "was what transpired between the two when they finally met."

"How do we know when that occurred?"

"Our cameras had Hess under observation as he wrote at his desk. At eight forty-seven, he rose and went over to the door that opens into the garden. The microphones recorded their conversation in the living room for—"

"Whose conversation?" Churchill asked.

"I beg your pardon?" Simon looked at Churchill, who eyed him steadily. This was the first time the prime minister had asked him that.

"You said you recorded their conversation. I asked you, 'Whose conversation?' "

John Simon blinked. How could he not have thought of that himself?

"Why, the conversation between Rudolf Hess and the reporter, naturally."

"Did you see the reporter on film?" Churchill asked.

"I see what you're getting at. It's true, our cameras don't reach that far. It's quite impossible to—"

"So, we're operating on assumption here."

"Surely, the nature of the conversation—"

"How did he identify himself?" Churchill asked. "The visitor, I mean."

"He called himself Ian MacDonald, and said he had been sent by Hamilton. There's no doubt as to his true identity. None whatso—"

"Precisely what did they discuss during their time in the living room?" Churchill resumed his pacing.

"The reporter questioned Hess about his treatment, what sort of information he was receiving from us, who his main contact was, that sort of thing."

"And Hess replied?"

"That he was dissatisfied with the level of communication, that he refused to accept our assessment of the war on the eastern front, even disputed the wireless reports."

Churchill paused again.

"He expressed his frustration to the visitor, in other words," he said.

Why did Churchill call him "the visitor"? Why did he refuse to acknowledge that he was the reporter from Glasgow? Was there any significance to that?

"His frustration, yes," Simon said, "and he queried the reporter about his reason for being there."

"Which was?"

"Again, that he'd been sent by Hamilton and wished to publicize the details of Hess's mission and needed his cooperation for that. He even suggested that they might be able to expedite his return to Germany."

Churchill said nothing. He stood in the center of the room, puffing on his cigar, lost in thought. Finally, he turned to Simon and said, "So here we get to the heart of the matter. Tell me, John, precisely what was Hess's response to that?"

Simon shifted uneasily in his chair. He cleared his throat, straightened his spine and said in as strong a voice as he could muster, "At that point, I'm afraid, the rest of the conversation was broken off. There were some muffled sounds in the room, whispered voices mostly incomprehensible, and . . . and then nothing."

Churchill looked down at Simon, furrowed his brow, jabbed his cigar in the air and said, "Nothing, John, nothing from that point on, which can only mean that they moved out of the room, beyond the reach of the microphones."

"Out of the flat," Simon said. "Our devices would have picked up a conversation anywhere on the premises. They could only have gone outside, into the garden. Hess obviously would expect us to have him under surveillance. They conducted the remainder of their meeting beyond earshot. What transpired is anybody's guess."

"Damn! Damn!" Churchill almost stamped his foot. "And from that moment on we know nothing of their conversation."

"I'm afraid not."

"And what of the visitor?" Churchill said. "I assume both he and the journal are in custody."

"They are. I'm expecting a full report from my field operative shortly."

"Yes, well, you'll fill me in immediately, of course."

"Of course."

"What's to become of the visitor?" Churchill said.

"That depends to a great extent on him," Simon said. "How much he knows and to what extent he's prepared to cooperate."

Churchill paced across the room, puffing absently on his cigar. He turned to Simon and said, "It's absolutely imperative that we have his full cooperation. Anything less simply will not do."

CHAPTER TWENTY-NINE

Jᴇɴɴʏ Wɪʟᴋɪɴs ᴘᴜsʜᴇᴅ the pram up Threadneedle Street, past faces as gray and bleak as the Liverpool sky. She stopped in front of number forty-eight, set the brake so the pram wouldn't roll and lifted little Harry into her arms. Shifting his weight to her left side, she reached down and gripped the pram with her right hand and pulled it up the steps behind her.

The old witch was at her window facing the street, as she always was, nothing else to do but snoop on everybody who passed by.

"Any word from 'im today?" the old woman asked.

"Not yet," Jenny said. "You'll be the first to know."

"Fat chance," the old woman said. " 'e's no better than the other one. They're all alike, if you ask me."

"Nobody's askin'," Jenny said and continued past.

On the second landing she set the pram down on the floor, pushed the key into the door lock and entered the flat. She carried Harry, who was still asleep, over to his crib and laid him down inside it. She undid the buttons on his coat first, took it off, then removed her own and pushed the pram into the corner. She walked over to the stove and turned the gas on under the kettle for tea.

There was a light knock on the door. She ignored it at first, but then there was a second and a third, louder than the first, so she walked over toward the sound.

"Who's there?" she said.

"Telegram," a voice said. "For Miss Jenny Wilkins from Philip Renfield."

Her hand flew out quicker than she could think and turned the doorknob. Before she could open it herself, the door crashed in on her and knocked her back into the room, where she fell against the table. Two men rushed into the flat. The first was kneeling above her, his hand hard over her mouth before she had a chance to open it. The second man slammed the door behind him and stood scanning the flat from left to right with quick eyes. The man above her had on a black turtleneck sweater and a navy watch cap pulled low on his forehead. His eyes were dark and mean. He could have been a dockworker except that his body was thin and hard, without an ounce of bloat on it.

"Are you Jenny Wilkins?" the man above her said. "Just nod your head."

He gave her just enough slack to move her head up and down.

"Good," he said. His mouth smiled but his eyes did not. They drilled into her with the force of blinding light.

"The little bloke's in the crib there," the other man said.

Jenny saw the knife flash in the second man's hand, and her eyes widened in alarm. She squirmed to get free, but the man's hands were like steel on her mouth and body.

"Nothin'll happen to 'im," the man above her said, "if you promise not to squeal when I let your mouth go. Nary a peep. One word and we'll cut 'im right proper. Agreed?"

Jenny nodded yes.

The man let go and stood up, his eyes still boring holes in her. "Onto your feet now," he said, and motioned toward the sofa.

Jenny got up, not daring to utter a sound, and sat down on the sofa where he had pointed. The second man stood by little Harry's crib, and Jenny could see the glinting blade from the corner of her eye. The first man grabbed a chair from the kitchen and sat directly in front of her, both hands resting on his knees. His stare did not waver.

"I'm goin' t' ask you some questions," he said, "and I want straight answers. Lie to me once and—" He nodded toward the crib. "D' you get my drift?"

Jenny nodded.

"This Renfield chap," the man said, "how much did 'e tell you? All of it now, nice and quick."

Jenny opened her mouth to speak, but her throat was frozen with terror. She stammered, then finally said, "Tell me? About what?"

"Don't play dumb," the man said. "You know what I'm talkin' about."

"You mean about . . . why he went away?"

The man nodded and continued to stare at her with those dark, mean eyes.

"Only that he was covering a story. He had to find out about some things Harry told him."

"What sorts of things? Let's have it now. We don't have all day."

"He wouldn't tell me everything," Jenny said, "because he said it would be too dangerous for me. All I know is that Harry told him something about a top-secret assignment he had down in Wales. But I don't know what it was."

The man interrogating Jenny looked over toward his partner by the crib, and said, "Do it, Al. She ain't cooperatin' like she should."

Jenny turned and saw him raise his knife high in the air over little Harry's crib, as though he were ready to plunge down with it. She opened her mouth to scream, but the first man clamped it shut with an iron hand before any sound could come out.

"You've got one more chance," he said. He turned her head in the direction of his partner, who stood there with his knife still raised, observing her with a fiendish grin. "Tell it all now," the first man said, letting go of her mouth.

"Please." Jenny raised her hands to her face and sobbed desperately, her whole body shaking. "I swear to you, I don't know any more than's in that letter. Philip deliberately wouldn't tell me. How can I make you believe me?"

"What letter?" the man said.

"Harry's letter. I showed it to Philip the first time he came."

"Go get it," the man said.

As though in a trance, Jenny rose on unsteady legs and went into the kitchen to get the letter she had put there for safekeeping. She had barely taken it from its hiding place when the man grabbed it from her. She watched him, her eyes wide with fear, as he read it.

"This is it?" the man said.

"That's all I know," Jenny said. "Philip said it had to do with a story he was covering, but he wouldn't tell me what about."

"Pathetic bloke," the man said.

"Who?"

"Harry. You're better off rid of 'im, I don't mind tellin' you." The man slipped the letter into his pocket.

Jenny thought she detected a touch of compassion in his eyes for the first time. "What's become of Philip?" she asked.

The hardness returned to his eyes as he looked at her. "That depends on 'im," he said.

"What do you mean?"

"What becomes of 'im depends on how well 'e cooperates. He did you a good turn not tellin' you more than 'e had to. Let's hope he exercises the same good sense where 'is own neck is concerned. Not one word about this visit, y' hear?"

Jenny nodded yes. "Please don't hurt Philip," she said.

The man turned away and nodded to his partner. Silently, they headed toward the door. The first man turned back and said, "Forget about this letter, lady, and forget you ever heard about any top-secret nonsense goin' on in Wales. Or we'll be back."

Then they were gone, their footsteps echoing in the hall-way.

CHAPTER THIRTY

Rudolf Hess had just settled down at his writing desk, when he heard three knocks on the door. He checked the clock on the wall overhead. Eight twenty-eight. Almost the same time the visitor had come the first evening. Could it be him again? So soon?

He pushed his chair back from the desk, and almost rushed over to the door. He stood listening a moment, but there was silence on the other side.

"Who is it?" he said.

"Ian MacDonald," a voice said softly.

Hess almost jumped with excitement.

"One moment," he said as he unlatched the lock and turned the handle.

No sooner had he done that than the door burst in on him, sending him reeling backward into the room. Two men charged through the doorway, followed by two soldiers with automatic rifles at the ready. Hess was about to speak when the first man across the threshold struck him in the pit of the stomach with his fist, knocking the wind from him as he fell to the floor. Hess tried to struggle to his feet, but the man kicked his legs out from under him before he could get up.

Hess tried to speak, but the intruder silenced him with a backhand slap across the face. The man smiled down at him with his mouth, but his eyes were cold and hard with no laughter in them. He was dressed in a black turtleneck sweater, steel-tipped boots and a dark blue navy watch cap pulled low on his forehead.

"Keep an eye on him, lads, while I have a look about," said the man to his companions.

He walked over to Hess's writing desk and picked up the fresh pages of manuscript that Rudolf Hess had composed since early afternoon. The writing was in German and meant nothing to him. The man looked down at Hess and said, "Quite the scribbler you are, ain't that so?"

Hess tried to speak, but the words did not come out easily through his swollen lips and aching jaw.

"Who . . . who are you? What are you doing here?"

"Hold 'im down while I have a look," the rough man said to his partner. The soldiers stood ten feet away with their rifles trained on Hess.

The second man moved behind Hess and pinned his hands. The rough man moved closer and lowered his face toward Hess's.

"Don't get the wrong idea," he said with his mirthless grin. "I'm goin' to cop a feel but don't think I'm bein' fresh. One hasty move outa you, though, and I'll break your bloody arms, that much I promise you."

The rough man reached inside the front of Hess's shirt and found what he was looking for at once. He pulled out a thin sheaf of paper, perhaps a dozen sheets or so, that Hess had filled with his scrawl during the days since his encounter with the visitor.

"Your filing system's a bit odd," the man said, "but it does make my job a lot easier, I'll say that much for it."

"Please," Hess said. There was terror in his eyes, all the fight knocked out of him. "What are you doing? Where is Ian MacDonald?"

"MacDonald?" the rough man said. "I don't believe I've had the pleasure."

"I would like to speak to the lord chancellor," Hess said. "He would not permit this sort of treatment."

"The lord chancellor, is it now?" The man scratched his chin and smiled at his partner. "Our Nazi friend 'ere travels in different circles than poor blokes like us. We don't often get to have tea with the likes of 'im."

"I must speak to your prime minister at once!" There was panic in Hess's voice.

"Now he's blatherin' about old Winnie himself," the man said. "Seems there's no end to his acquaintances."

The rough man stood up, had one last look around the flat, and said, "Well, lads, we've found what we came for. Let's haul 'im off now, shall we?"

Hess's eyes opened wide, the fear a living presence in them. "Where are you taking me?" he said.

"It's off to the lockup now," the rough man said. "No more fancy livin' for *you* anymore. No more music and gardens, no more pretty pictures and no more paper and ink, that's for sure. Just a plain old cement lockup where we can keep an eye on you good an' proper. Let's go, lads."

CHAPTER THIRTY-ONE

THE SKY OVER Berlin was slate gray. Rain had pounded the city for a week without letup, and there was no sign it would end anytime soon. Inside Nazi headquarters, the atmosphere was equally oppressive. General Hiroshi Oshima sat rigidly at the long conference table across from Hitler and Ribbentrop. His translator and half a dozen aides sat beside him, but Hitler had summoned only one translator of his own for the occasion. Oshima could not help noticing how ludicrous the great German emperor looked in his long coat and tiny mustache, not like a warrior at all. Ribbentrop, by contrast, was poised and imperious, every inch a leader.

". . . We therefore urge you," Hitler read from a statement he held in his right hand, "to declare war without delay against both England and the United States."

Hitler sat down formally while Oshima's translator finished interpreting his words. The Japanese general sat still for a time, measuring the German leader carefully with eyes that gave nothing away. Finally, he spoke.

"Is Your Excellency indicating," he said, "that a state of actual war is to be established between Germany and the United States?"

Hitler did not reply immediately. Ribbentrop shifted in his seat, then raised his right forefinger.

"If I may," Ribbentrop said. "Roosevelt is a fanatic, totally unpredictable. It is impossible for Germany to anticipate what he will do next."

Oshima stared at Ribbentrop, then at the Führer, who glared back at him without speaking.

"Forgive me, but that is not what I asked," Oshima said. "Is Japan to understand, then, that Germany is now in a state of war with the United States?"

Hitler did not waste a second this time. He brought the flat of his hand down hard on the table, and said, "If Japan should engage in hostilities with the United States, Germany will join in as her ally at once. Without restraints."

"There is absolutely no question," Ribbentrop added, "of Germany's making a separate peace with the United States under those circumstances. The Führer is determined on this point."

Oshima settled back in his seat and permitted himself a tight smile for the first time. Even as they spoke, a carrier task force with Japanese bombers was en route to Pearl Harbor. As far as he was concerned, the matter had already been decided—with or without the Führer's cooperation.

"It is understood, then," Oshima said.

CHAPTER THIRTY-TWO

Sir John Simon sat in his study, trying to concentrate on the report in his lap. For twenty minutes now, he had not been able to read beyond the third or fourth sentence. Each time he tried to move along, his mind wandered to other matters, most particularly to the startling series of events of the past week.

A fire blazed in the hearth to his left, sending flashes of reddish light dancing across the pages. A lamp in the far corner cast its own dim glow throughout the oak-paneled library. All in all, it was a tranquil setting suited perfectly for an erudite man at his leisure, but there was no tranquility in John Simon's heart tonight. Finally, at precisely twenty minutes past eight, he heard the knock on the door that he had been waiting for all evening.

"Yes," he said.

"Your guest's arrived, sir," the butler said.

"Show him in."

"At once, sir."

Two minutes later a tall, lean man entered the study. His eyes were dark and glittering, and he was dressed in a black turtleneck sweater and a black leather coat. There was something about his attire that made him look as though he were dressed for business rather than for a leisurely stroll through the English mist.

"Will that be all, sir?" the butler said.

"Yes, Charles, you can leave us alone now. I'll show the gentleman out myself later."

"Very good, sir."

Simon studied his guest for a moment after the butler left, and forced a joyless smile to his lips.

"Sit down." Simon motioned toward a leather chair across from his own. "Some brandy?"

"I could do with a drop, sir, thank you very much."

Simon poured generous portions into two snifters from a decanter on the sideboard, handed one to his guest and sat down.

"I daresay you've been quite busy these past few days," Simon said.

The man smiled and the look was chilling.

"You might say that, yes indeed, sir."

"Any problems?"

"Nary a one. Smooth as silk it went, just as we planned."

"The girl?"

"Doesn't know a thing. Won't be any trouble from her, sir."

John Simon sipped his brandy, then swallowed it with a gulp. His eyes glittered in the firelight.

"And Hess?" he said.

"He won't be communicating with anyone for a long time. Caught him at his desk, we did, scribbling away for all 'e was worth."

"You took the pages?"

"Brought them with me, sir, along with the others."

"Ah, yes." Simon paused and looked at his brandy some-what distastefully and put it down. How Churchill could drink so much of it was beyond him. "Speaking of that, you had no trouble with the reporter?"

"None, sir." The man's eyes shone in the dimly lit room, and the smile on his face was almost a grimace. "We followed him from the 'otel and kept on his trail all the way up the hill. Waited out there half the day and part of the night. It was no picnic out there in the cold, I can tell you that, sir."

"I don't imagine it was."

"Anyway, we waited until he came outside with Hess."

"Yes?"

"They chatted out there in the garden a while, a good quarter hour or so I'd say."

"Go on."

"Hess gave it to him from inside his shirt, just as you said he might."

John Simon sat still in his chair. His eyes were fixed in-tently on his guest. If he was feeling anything inside, it did not show in his eyes.

"Then what did you do?" he asked.

"Waited for him in the woods, just beyond the—"

"The gazebo, yes?"

"He started back around the grounds, the way he came, and that's when we jumped him, sir."

"Was there a struggle, any sounds that might've been heard?"

"Oh no, sir. Took 'im totally by surprise. T'was no sound a'tall, sir."

"You've brought him with you?" Simon said.

"He's downstairs now, sir, just as you asked."

"So it's done then. Good work, Tom. You've brought the notebook with you?"

"Have it right here, sir." Tom reached inside his leather coat and pulled out Hess's notebook, which he handed to Simon.

"The new pages too?" Simon asked.

"It's all there, sir."

Simon stared down at the document in his hands as though it were a sacred scroll. "Well done," he said.

"It's all in a day's work, as they say, sir."

"Indeed."

John Simon reached inside his lounging coat and removed a bulky envelope filled with Bank of England notes of various denominations. He handed it to Tom.

"This is for you," he said. "You've gone far beyond the call of duty this time."

"Thank you, sir." Tom's smile was broad, his dark eyes bright.

"You've earned it," Simon said. "Lord knows, you've earned it. Bring him in now, then you can go."

JOHN SIMON OBSERVED the sandy-haired reporter as he entered his study. The man looked thin, weary and bedraggled. Despite all that, however, there was a spark in his eyes. It was the look of a man who had been beaten down, but not defeated. John Simon did not stand up. He sat quite still in his fine leather chair and stared at the visitor. Then he said, "Mr. Renfield, I presume."

The visitor nodded yes and glared at Simon.

"Have a seat, Mr. Renfield." Simon motioned toward the chair to his right. "May I offer you a spot of brandy?"

Philip looked at the decanter on the table beside Simon, then at Simon's half-filled snifter.

"I would like that. Thank you," he said.

Simon poured two inches of brandy into a snifter and handed it to Philip, who breathed in its bouquet, sipped it slowly and said, "It's quite good, thank you."

"I'll get right to the point," Simon said. "You've caused us no end of grief with this snooping of yours. What did you expect to accomplish, if you don't mind my asking?"

"I'm a reporter, sir," Philip said without hesitation. "My job is to seek out the truth and report it to the public as best as I know how."

"Indeed," Simon said. He sniffed his own glass, crinkled his nose and put it down without drinking. "And what truths have you uncovered, Mr. Renfield?"

"Unfortunately, I was—deterred from completing my job. The truth remains a mystery to me."

"You weren't hurt?" There was genuine concern in Simon's voice.

"No broken bones, sir, nothing like that. Your men, if that's who they were, used just the right amount of force to do the job."

Simon offered a half smile and studied his visitor. "Just how much do you know, Mr. Renfield?"

"Not nearly as much as I'd like to," Philip said. "Only that Rudolf Hess's plane crashed in Scotland and he parachuted to safety. He was apparently expected by the Duke of Hamilton for a reason I have not yet been able to determine. A double was put in the Tower of London for public viewing while the real Hess was transported, first to a safe house in Glasgow, and later to a sanatorium in Wales. There he kept a journal that the government was anxious to get hold of. Beyond that, I know very little."

"Regarding Hess's association with the Duke of Hamilton," Simon said, "you must have arrived at some conclusions following your conversation with the man."

Philip did not reply immediately. It seemed to Simon as if

he were wrestling with his thoughts, trying to reconstruct the events of that evening, trying to remember how much of the conversation took place in Hess's quarters and how much in the garden, beyond the range of any hidden microphones.

"Hess seemed to believe," Philip finally said, "that the U.K. and Germany had some sort of a common destiny, that our country and his should be working together instead of attempting to destroy each other. That was as specific as he got. I can only assume that he wanted to get that message across to the highest levels of our government."

Simon observed Philip thoughtfully. Apparently he had decided to be honest, Simon thought, and tell all he knew. Surely Hess would not have revealed the details of any formal agreement between the two countries to a man he had just met for the first time, a stranger to whom he had spoken for no longer than a half hour in all. Renfield had been effective in winning Hess's confidence sufficiently to have gained possession of the journal. He was quite an ingenious young fellow, not quite as young as he first appeared, obviously intelligent and dedicated to his calling. He could be very useful—if only his reason and sense of proportion matched his craftiness.

"Mr. Renfield," Simon said, "I'm quite impressed by you, I mean that sincerely. You're obviously highly inventive, dedicated, persistent, intelligent. Those are all excellent traits.

"I'm going to be straightforward with you. This entire Hess incident is most embarrassing to our government and our nation. We did not welcome Hess's visit, nor—aside from certain elements in our society—were we interested in any messages he wanted to deliver. This is extremely unfortunate, and the sooner it's swept aside and forgotten, the better for all.

"I'm going to make you a proposition. You're to drop this quest of yours at once. Your pursuit of any so-called truths regarding the Hess affair has run its course. Your talents and skills can be put to far better use than they have until now. You can be of great service to both yourself and your country if you agree to cooperate with us."

Philip sipped his brandy and stared at Simon. "I don't understand," he said.

"I'm offering you a job, Mr. Renfield," Simon said, "a very important post putting your talents to work for your country. I'm in a position to make life quite comfortable for you."

Philip smiled but his eyes did not. He said, "Sounds more like a bribe to me, if you don't mind my being blunt, sir."

"It is not in your interests to be difficult, Mr. Renfield. You've nowhere else to turn. We've been in touch with your father-in-law, and he has agreed to cut you loose. You no longer have a job at the newspaper, Mr. Renfield, nor any other means of support. Hess's journal is now in our possession, so you've no proof of anything if, indeed, such proof even exists. You've nothing to go on but surmise and speculation. Who's going to believe any theories you may develop? Where's your documentation? You've nothing, sir. Your investigation has reached an impasse. It's over."

Philip smiled openly now. He finished off his brandy. He said, "I believe in our form of government, sir, because it has staunchly defended democratic institutions and concepts, including freedom of the press. Without those freedoms, sir, are we any better than the people we're fighting?"

"This is wartime!" There was exasperation and impatience in Simon's tone. "We are a bastion of freedom and democracy, but not Utopia. It doesn't exist. Politics is the art of coping with reality. I will not debate with you. Do you accept my offer, Mr. Renfield?"

"How long do I have to decide?" Philip said.

"I'm a patient man, but patience has its limits. Take a week if you like."

"And if I decide against it?"

Simon drained his glass and looked directly into Philip's eyes. He said, "You will be utterly and totally on your own, Renfield. Thoroughly cut off from everything."

"Thank you for being candid with me, sir. How do I contact you?"

"We will contact you. In a week. Of course we will know where you are, and what you are doing all the while."

CHAPTER THIRTY-THREE

Searchlights illuminated the midnight sky beyond the prime minister's window. They circled the heavens in sweeping arcs, catching the rolling mist in their beams. The mist shone, heavy and thick like a physical presence.

Inside, the prime minister waited impatiently. He did not like to be kept waiting by anyone, let alone one of his subordinates. He checked his watch. Ten past twelve. Simon should have been here twenty minutes ago. What was keeping him?

Finally a knock.

"John? Is that you?" called the prime minister.

"Yes. Sorry I'm late."

Churchill opened the door and Simon entered the room. He was looking remarkably fresh for this hour of the night, more rested than he had in weeks.

"What kept you?" Churchill said.

"Some last-minute business. I left as quickly as I could."

"Well, come in, come in. Sit near the fire, if you like. Brandy?"

"Thanks, no. I'll be up half the night."

"Some sherry, then." It was not a question. The prime minister filled his brandy tumbler halfway up and poured a measure of sherry in a cordial glass, which he handed to Simon. Simon looked at it a moment, then accepted it and sat down in the easy chair by the fire.

"So, it's finally happening." Churchill moved in front of Simon's chair and turned toward him. "The Yanks will be in it before long."

"Perhaps not. They still have time to shore up their defenses. The Japanese may well have to abandon their plans now."

"We shall see," Churchill said. "The tide seems to be turning now."

"So it seems," Simon said. "Hitler's done the impossible and lost every advantage he started with."

"Incredible, isn't it?" Churchill sat down opposite Simon and looked into his glass, swirled it, took a swallow. "I can't remember any military commander in history forfeiting such overwhelming odds. Why do you think he waited so long?"

"So long?"

"Before advancing on Moscow. Seems to me that should have been his key target from the start. Once Moscow fell, the entire country would have been demoralized."

"It doesn't make any sense to me," Simon said. "His generals had the correct strategy from the beginning, but he overruled them at every turn."

"The man's mad, John, there's no other explanation for it."

"I should think that goes without saying. Lord knows, you gave him all . . ."

Simon hesitated.

"You were about to say, John?"

"Only that he had nothing to fear on his western flank, nothing whatsoever to divert him from his objective in the east."

"Ah, yes." Churchill looked at the fire, then back at Simon. "As long as we're on that subject, I've just finished reading the journal. What do you think?"

Simon raised the sherry glass to his lips and sipped slowly. His face was as expressionless as it had been since he arrived.

"It's as we expected," Simon said. "Hitler never had any intention of leaving us alone after the war. He remains determined to conquer us, and eventually the entire world if he can. The journal is filled mostly with blather about Nazi history and philosophy. Ravings of a fanatic.

"The great prize, of course," Simon continued, "is Hess's revelation about the pending Japanese attack on the Americans that you alluded to before. Pearl Harbor in the Hawaiian Islands. I assume you've alerted Roosevelt about it while there's still time to take action?"

Churchill stared down at the brandy lying still in his snifter. For an interminable moment there was no sound in the room, only the ticking of a clock on the wall. Churchill drew an audible breath, swirled his brandy and inhaled deeply.

"I'm not sure that's wise, John," Churchill said. "We have no way of knowing for sure if the information is reliable."

"But surely they should be put on notice." Simon's eyes were wide with alarm. "I mean, what if—"

"There are so many variables in the picture, John," Churchill said. "We have no way of knowing anything for certain except the facts at hand. Everything else is speculation that will only serve to alarm our friends."

"Dear Lord." Simon was visibly shaken, more so than he had ever been in a lifetime of public service. "It's good we made the effort to see what was in the journal. You've destroyed it, I assume."

"It's been taken care of," Churchill said. "As far as that other matter is concerned, what have you heard from the reporter, John?"

"His deadline's up tomorrow. We'll be talking to him first thing in the morning."

"What do you think?"

"There's no question in my mind," Simon said, "that he'll do the right thing."

"And if he doesn't?" asked the prime minister.

Sir John Simon shrugged his shoulders and finished his sherry in a gulp. "What has to be done will be done," he said. "We're all responsible for our actions in the end, aren't we?"

CHAPTER THIRTY-FOUR

December 1941

ADOLF HITLER SAT in the corner of his tiny room in the Wolf's Lair, staring into space. Perspiration rolled freely down his ashen cheeks, and his eyes were hollow craters in the darkness. Despite the heat and the stuffiness of the close quarters, his tunic was buttoned up to his neck.

The news from the eastern front was not good. Tanks were mired in the mud, rain and sleet, and swirling snow fell without letup. Temperatures plunged overnight to twenty and thirty degrees below zero. Soldiers of the Reich lay shivering in their foxholes, demoralized, sick with fever, unprepared for the harsh Russian winter. All thoughts of advance, of even holding ground that had been fought for and won, were out of the question.

There was a knock on the bunker door, but Hitler did not respond. More dispatches from the front, more bad news.

A second knock. Hitler stirred. His eyes flickered in the darkness. A third knock.

"Yes?" Hitler's voice was barely audible.

"A dispatch, Führer." The voice belonged to Oberleutnant Heim.

"More news from the front?"

"No, Führer. A message from Dietrich, regarding the Pacific."

Hitler stirred, his eyes coming alive. He sat upright in his chair.

"Bring it to me," he said.

Heim entered the stuffy room and handed the dispatch to the Führer. Hitler read it through, quickly the first time, then more slowly. After he finished reading it through for the third time, he looked up at Heim and said, "Is this report correct?"

"I believe so, Führer. I asked for confirmation from Dietrich before I brought it to you, and he said he received confirmation himself by telephone."

Hitler's mood changed dramatically. He shot out of his chair and began pacing across the room, brushing Heim lightly as he passed. He checked his watch. It was 4:17 in the afternoon, December 7. The Japanese had been true to their word. Their attack had been swift and clean and timely, right to the precise hour of the day.

"Take this down," Hitler said. "Send dispatches at once to Keitel, Jodl and Reichenau. 'Take courage, stop. It is done as said, stop. We cannot lose, stop. We now have a partner who has not been defeated in three thousand years, stop. Your Supreme Commander, Adolf Hitler.' "

CHAPTER THIRTY-FIVE

October 1946

PHILIP RENFIELD SCANNED the front page of the *Times* as he sipped his morning coffee in his study. The papers were filled with news of the Nuremberg trials, and the story that interested him most was the one concerning Rudolf Hess.

HESS SENTENCED TO LIFE IN PRISON
Deputy Führer of Germany to be Transported To Spandau Prison in Berlin

Philip shook his head from side to side and drained the last of the lukewarm coffee. So much for the Hess affair now, he thought. Hess had been kept in total isolation throughout the remainder of the war, and he would most likely be subjected to the same fate for the rest of his life. No one would ever get near him, ever have a private word with him, Philip was convinced. There was no question in his mind that Churchill had accommodated Hitler as he launched his blitzkrieg against Russia. Why else had it taken Britain two and a half years, following Hess's landing in Scotland, to begin a full-scale operation against Germany?

There was a light rap on the door, and Philip looked up from his paper. "Yes?" he said.

"It's me, darling. May I come in?"

"Of course."

Jenny looked smashing today, as usual. Her hair, longer now than when he first met her, was parted on the side and swept over into a dip across the right side of her face, Veronica Lake style. Her blue dress hugged her lovely figure in just the right places, showing off the curve of her hips and her thighs to full advantage. It was her legs, Philip had decided long ago, and her sweet vulnerability that endeared her to him most.

"You look lovely, Jenny," he said.

"You're sweet." She came over to where he was sitting and kissed him on the forehead.

"You're off, are you?" he said.

"I've a meeting with Harry's headmaster, then lunch with the ladies. I'll be back two-thirtyish or so."

"Enjoy yourself," he said. "Say hello for me. No problem with the boy, is there?"

"Just the usual antics. Nothing too serious this time, I don't think. Will you be here when I get back?"

"I've a luncheon for Sir John," Philip said. "His retirement affair. Then I'm off to see my publisher."

"How exciting for you, love," Jenny said. "Your first novel, what you've always wanted."

"Yes, well, there may be some problem with the censorship board. It's time they disbanded the bloody thing. There's no excuse for it now that the war's over."

Philip's novel, *The Journal*, a fictionalized account of Rudolf Hess's landing in Scotland, was due out in the spring—if it passed review.

"Yes, well I'm sure it'll work out fine, love."

"If it's not one thing it's another," Philip said. He reached out and squeezed her hand. "I guess we shouldn't complain, though. Life's been pretty good to us these past few years. Better than for most."

Jenny ran her fingers through his hair, now beginning to gray somewhat on the sides and thin out on top. She said, "You're not sorry you did it, are you, love?"

Philip did not respond immediately. Not sorry he—sold out? Why not say it honestly? Well, he wasn't the first to do so, nor would he be the last. He had gone to work for the government and dropped the Hess business. Sir John had kept his word, rewarded him handsomely for work that, in Philip's view, was a perversion of his talents.

"No, I'm not sorry." He swept his hand in an arc to encompass the room. "If one has to sell out, one might as well do it in style."

"Hush, love," Jenny said. "Don't be hard on yourself. Anyone would've done the same under the circumstances. Besides, you've got your novel now. You'll have the last word in the end."

"Perhaps." Philip smiled up at her. He stood up and took her in his arms. "You've made it all worthwhile, my darling. Having you, being able to make a home for you and Harry— that's what's important to me. And you're right, I do have my book. And it *will* be published. I'll be damned if I'll let anybody stop me from telling my story again."

"I'm so happy with you, Philip." Jenny kissed him passionately. "And I want you to be happy too. You've every right to be."

"I am." Philip smiled down at her, patted her rump. "You'd better be off before I make you late for your appointment. See you later, darling."

Jenny kissed him again, and then she was off. He watched her leave the room, listened to her footsteps in the hall. The driver was at the curb, ready for her with the door open.

Through the bay window that opened into the courtyard, he saw her get into the car, watched it leave the curb and take her off to do her rounds.

It was a good life, Philip thought. Money. Prestige. Love. Now his book. What more could he ask for? If they blocked it here, he could bring it out in the United States first, let the Yanks have first crack at it. He enjoyed weaving his fiction. Through it he could create a truer reality, one more telling and more incisive than the world perceived through the senses. Or so he told himself.

Perhaps it was not such a terrible compromise after all.

EPILOGUE

August 1987

From the outside, Spandau Prison is a dismal red brick building located in what was called for many years after the war the British section of East Berlin. Built more than a century ago, it contains enough cells for 600 prisoners, an execution chamber with facilities for hanging eight people at a time from hooks suspended from the ceiling, as well as a French-style guillotine.

During the war, Spandau was a preserve of the Gestapo where wealthy Jewish merchants were tortured until they revealed the location of their money and possessions before they were sent to concentration camps further to the east. Rudolf Hess had no way of knowing, when he set out on that flight to Scotland in May 1941, that he would spend the last forty-one years of his life at Spandau, separated from those he loved and honored the most.

Three times he attempted to take his own life rather than live in confinement and disgrace; three times he failed. Over the years he saw his fellow prisoners released after serving their sentences or, in some cases, for health reasons. His last companion and fellow prisoner, Albert Speer, was released in 1966. After that Hess lived alone, the last remaining prisoner at Spandau.

Speer had been his confidant. It was to him Hess confided that his apparent amnesia was a pretense, a psychological ruse he adopted to avoid intense interrogation—possibly even the gallows. The most difficult part of all had been the pretense of not recognizing old friends and colleagues, even family members, when they were brought in by the doctors to jog his memory. He had even gone so far as to stare blankly at Ilse and his son Wolf during their brief visits as though they were total strangers. Despite it all, he had failed to obtain the early release in the custody of his family, on grounds of insanity, that he hoped for.

Among the wartime allies, the Russians had been the most difficult for Hess to deceive. Through the years they had made it quite clear that they did not believe in his insanity. They were the most relentless in their questioning, badgering him incessantly for information about his wartime mission to Scotland. Hess refused to be moved. He stared down his crude interrogators with their coarse, heavy faces, and dared them to break him. He was the most disciplined of all the Nazis, the most strong-willed except for the Führer.

He would have preferred an honorable death by his own hand to this interminable captivity, but his attempts had failed. Now, as he was contemplating a fourth, Ilse had managed to convey to him during her last fifteen-minute visit that there was a good chance he might be released soon. Even the most ardent anti-Nazis thought that after forty-six years of captivity, five in England during the war and the last forty-one in Spandau, he deserved to be moved to more livable quarters. He was ninety-three years of age and his health was failing. There was agitation for his release from many quarters, not just Germany, and Ilse was convinced that it was only a question of time before he would be free to live out the rest of his life with her at home.

But Hess did not respond. He still pretended not to recognize his wife or the words she spoke, and he gave no outward sign of understanding her.

INWARDLY HESS WAS jubilant. Finally there was hope after all these years.

Hope!

If the gods were good to him they would grant him just enough time to tell his story to the world. The secret of his mission. So everyone would understand. Perhaps there would be enough time to reconstruct his journal, his document for posterity, his tribute to the Führer and the ideals for which they fought. How glorious! Heil Hitler! My Führer, you will be vindicated in the end! There was no question of taking his own life now. His mission was not yet completed.